An Ellery Queen Mystery

THE PERFECT CRIME

BY ELLERY QUEEN

Based on the Columbia Motion Picture
ELLERY QUEEN AND THE PERFECT CRIME

GROSSET & DUNLAP

Publishers   NEW YORK

Copyright, 1942, by
GROSSET & DUNLAP, INC.

Designed and produced by Artists and Writers Guild, Inc.

Printed in the United States of America

CONTENTS

CHAPTER		PAGE
I	Prelude to Crime	1
II	Fair Warning	13
III	The Voice of Death	28
IV	Murder	40
V	Miss Emerson	53
VI	Clues	66
VII	Money Talks	79
VIII	Mystery House	95
IX	An Unromantic Proposal	108
X	Shyster	117
XI	Cherchez la Femme	130
XII	Confession	143
XIII	Roundup	156
XIV	The Murder Again	173
XV	Dictation	192

THE PERFECT CRIME

CHAPTER I

Prelude to Crime

Ellery Queen looked at the mahogany basket marked out on the corner of his desk, and he frowned. It contained three chapters of his latest book. They were ready for retyping, and yet he had foolishly let Nikki Porter, his secretary, talk him into giving her the morning off. The absence of the sound of clicking typewriter keys in the outer office was a constant reminder of Nikki's persuasiveness—or his own weakness. But Nikki could talk you into about anything.

Ellery scowled at the portable typewriter before him on the mahogany desk, his silver eyes half closed. Leaning back, he stretched his long legs and gave himself over to thought.

The furrows of his frown deepened into a scowl as he heard a noise coming from the outer office. Someone was tapping on the glass panel of the hall door with a key or a silver coin. The *rat-tat-tat* continued as Ellery got up and, crossing his private office, went towards the door that, seen from the inside, proclaimed in gilt letters ᴎɟɟu϶ ʏяɹɹɹ. Why had he given Nikki the morning off? For a permanent wave! He remembered Nikki's plaintive expression as, looking in the mirror of her compact, she smoothed back her golden-brown hair. "But Monsieur Paul can only take me at—" Monsieur Paul!

He jerked the door open.

"Hello, El. You can't fool me—I knew you were in. I heard you typing." The dark-eyed young man standing in the hall grinned disarmingly. "Sorry if I'm interrupting. But I've got to see you. No kidding."

"All right, come in, Walt," Ellery said resignedly. He led the way back to his office.

Walter Mathews was tall, with Charles Boyer eyes and black hair—that two-legged miracle—a man's man whom women liked. Ellery had known him for three years and, while sometimes he had been momentarily exasperated by Walter's excessive self-confidence, Ellery laid the blame at other doors. At twenty-one Walter Mathews had come into the inheritance his mother had left in trust for him when she died ten years before, and instantly a college boy had become a millionaire. But Walter was naturally generous and friendly, and his genuine good nature more than offset his occasional highhandedness with less fortunate mortals.

As he dropped into the chair beside Ellery Queen's desk, he took a deep breath.

"Asthma," Ellery asked, "or love?"

Walter looked darkly at Ellery. Then his quick smile flashed. But the smile disappeared as he said, "I've had the devil of a row with Uncle John."

"Again?" Ellery pushed his silver cigarette case across the desk.

Walter shook his head at the extended case and continued to glower.

"This one was *finis*. I've cleared out for good. Temporarily I'm living at the Yale Club, if you want to get hold of me. This time I told the old boy exactly what I think of him! Rhodes cooked up this dirty deal, but I think Uncle John double-crossed Rhodes, too. There's some satisfaction in that. But he's ruined Ray Garten. That's what burns me up." Suddenly a look of real anger came into Walter's eyes. "He ought to have his neck broken!"

"Here, calm your leaping soul," Ellery Queen said soothingly. "You're not being particularly lucid. Who's Rhodes? Is Garten your fiancée's father? And what's it all about?"

Walter leaned forward.

"Yes, Raymond Garten, Marian's father," he said grimly. "I've come to you about him. You're the only person I know I can trust in this. Rhodes is a lawyer—used to be a corporation lawyer, but I guess he was a little obvious even for a corporation. He has a private practice now, anyway. He and Uncle John are thick as blood-brothers. Naturally. Dear Uncle Johnny's never made a cent honestly in his life."

"There are better reputations in Wall Street," Ellery nodded. Walter's uncle was a plunger with a genius for unloading at the right time. The uncanny consistency with which he slithered out from under stock issues just before they crashed had given him an unsavory reputation even among the most realistic brokers; and although his surface operations were unquestionably legal, there were underground rumors about his skill at bribery.

"Well, his reputation is finished now, whatever it was," Walter snapped. "Not that he gives a darn. Money's all he cares about, and he's passed the fifty-million mark, so I suppose even he's satisfied. He cleaned up over ten millions in Chickawassi Petroleum."

Ellery blinked. Not long before he had read in the papers about the Chickawassi debacle and the subsequent agitation for an investigation by the district attorney's office. But no action had been taken, and the papers had already dropped the story.

"Was John Mathews mixed up in *that*?"

Walter grunted.

"He engineered the whole crooked business, through Rhodes. But you won't hear Uncle John's name connected with it officially—only as a stockholder. Rhodes did all the dirty work. It's the old game. The company leases hundreds of miles of land that geologists say is oil-bearing. Then they start test wells. They get oil, all right—enough oil to start promoting the stock. It's not listed on the big board. It's dealt in over the counter. That makes it easier. They run the stock up from ten cents a share to a hundred and thirty-five dollars. Then all the new holes they drill come in dry. But before that bit of information leaks out, Uncle John unloads. The price of the stock falls to zero, of course, when the bad news reaches the public. Then another dummy holding company buys up all the shares for nothing and a year or two later starts operations again. You see, the first company stops drilling a hundred feet above the oil bed and calls it a dry hole. The new organization, which of course is another of Uncle John's dummies, drills the extra hundred feet and strikes it rich."

"Very neat," said Ellery, dryly. "But why bring the harrowing details to me? The D.A.'s the man you want to see."

Walter grunted again.

"You mean that's what the stockholders ought to do. I agree with you, but I'm not a stockholder, thank Heaven! And the district attorney probably wouldn't get anywhere. He couldn't get anything on Uncle John—the worst he could be charged with is being a shrewd operator. And Rhodes isn't an officer of the company, either—just an outside attorney who drew up the articles of incorporation and so forth. Besides, even if they could prove anything it would be too late to save Marian's father."

Ellery Queen looked quickly at Walter.

"Save him? Is Garten involved in this, too?"

"He isn't 'involved.' He's ruined. Dear Unkie John has ruined him."

"But I thought Garten was enormously rich."

"He was well off once, never 'enormously' rich. For years he's been investing in rare books. It's his hobby."

"Hobby, my hat!" Ellery scowled. "It's a good lot more than a hobby. Raymond Garten is supposed to have one of the finest private libraries in America."

"Yes, he has," Walter agreed. "It's not so large—only three or four thousand books. But some of them are terribly rare and valuable—they cost him a fortune. It's his lifework. He even mortgaged the house to buy some of them. I guess things were getting pretty bad. But he thought he saw a chance to recoup in the Chickawassi business. Uncle John fed him hook, line, and sinker; and he bit. Mr. Garten put in everything he had—he even borrowed from his bank. Two hundred thousand, I believe. He's wiped out—clean."

Ellery frowned as he tapped his cigarette in the jade ash tray.

"Did your uncle know that you're engaged to Marian Garten?"

"Of course he knew."

"Then why didn't he tip Garten off when to sell out?"

"Tip him off!" Walter thumped the desk with his fist. "The slimy old crook told Mr. Garten that everything was O.K. even after he'd started unloading himself! He didn't want the market to break too fast. Not till he got out."

"You're sure of that?"

"Listen," said Walter, clenching his fists. "The other day Uncle John left the safe open in the library when he went upstairs for a few minutes. I got my nose in it and pawed around until I found what I was looking for. A telegram dated the tenth from Chickawassi, Oklahoma. It said, 'Discontinuing operations noon fifteenth per instructions.' The tenth was three weeks ago. It was on the fifteenth that the rumors began, and Garten called up to find out if there was anything to them. I know personally that Uncle John told him to hang on, that everything was all right, and to forget it. Mr. Garten was worried too because some of his friends had bought Chickawassi because he did. Even the Garten librarian got nipped for his savings, for instance. Uncle John burned *him* for five thousand bucks."

"But why would Mr. Mathews play such a trick on the father of the girl you're going to marry? Or is he beyond even family loyalty?"

"Loyalty! He never heard the word," Walter said contemptuously. "Besides, he doesn't want me to marry Marian. He doesn't like her. He'd be tickled to death if this breaks up the match."

"Why does he disapprove?"

"Lord only knows. Perhaps because she went to college. He doesn't approve of girls having an education. Then he's always had a grudge against Garten because the Gartens built their house directly behind ours. It partly blocks our view of the river. But someone would have built there. Too bad it wasn't an apartment house. Well, whatever the reason, I think he deliberately tricked Mr. Garten and hoped that it would break our engagement."

"And did it?"

"No, of course not," Walter said indignantly. "Marian's been perfectly swell, and so has Mr. Garten.

They're taking the whole thing like thoroughbreds. But I really believe that if he has to sell his library it will pretty nearly kill the old man."

"How old is he?"

"Well, he's past fifty."

"Old! Does he have to sell the library?"

"Ellery, Garten's so blamed honorable that he leans over backwards. He's doing it to pay off his creditors. The books are to be auctioned this afternoon, the house furnishings later. They moved into an apartment last week."

"It must be hard for him at his time of life," Ellery said thoughtfully.

"Ghastly. His lifework going under the auctioneer's hammer. It's a crime to break up that collection." He set his jaws. "That's where you come in."

"Me?" Ellery raised his brows. "You've declared *me* in in this drama of Good vs. Evil?"

Walter tossed a check on Ellery's desk.

Ellery, who was sprawled back in his chair, sat up quickly and looked at the check: "Ellery Queen. Two hundred and fifty thousand dollars and no cents. Walter Mathews."

Slowly Ellery raised his eyes.

"If I correctly follow the workings of your so-called mind," he murmured, "you want Mr. Ellery Queen to sit in at the auction sale."

Walter nodded.

"That's the inventory appraisal figure, so it's probably more than you'll need. I want you to bid in every book that's put up. The Garten collection is going to be my engagement present to Marian. She'll have to persuade her father to take care of it for the rest of his life. Ellery, you'll do it?"

Ellery caressed his lean jaw lightly, and grinned.

"I'd be honored." He whistled a long note. "Two hundred and fifty grand! But why don't you bid them in yourself?"

"Mr. Garten wouldn't stand for it. He'll be there. He'd have me thrown out. You don't know the old boy's pride. When I offered to make good his losses on Chickawassi, he told me where to get off. He says it was a straight business deal and he has to pay for his lack of foresight."

"When's the sale?" Ellery asked briskly.

"This afternoon. You *will* do it, Ellery?"

Ellery grinned.

"For one hour I'll know what it feels like to be a millionaire. News item: Ellery Queen buys Garten Collection for $250,000. Wait till Dad sees it in the papers! Wait till old Doc Prouty sees it—and Sergeant Velie!" Ellery shook with laughter. "Certainly I'll do it!"

"Swell! We'd better beat it over to your bank and deposit the check. I had it certified, as you see," Walter said. "Give the auctioneer *your* check. My name mustn't appear, Ellery."

"I hope the teller at my bank doesn't die of shock when he sees this immortal document. Just a moment, Walter."

Ellery scribbled on a pad of paper:

Sec. Porter, type stuff in 'out' basket. Stay till six to make up some of the time you've wasted. I've gone to the Raymond Garten auction to buy Garten Collection. I think I can snap it up for about $250,000—or even less, maybe. Ta-ta! E.Q.

CHAPTER II

Fair Warning

"Thirty-five dollars bid. Thirty-five dollars. Do I hear forty? Thirty-five dollars." The auctioneer paused to look incredulously at the faces before him. "An 1865 edition of *Alice's Adventures in Wonderland*. A first edition, ladies and gentlemen," he repeated for the tenth time. "Do you know—"

"Forty dollars," said a dreamy voice, the voice of a gentleman named Queen.

"Forty dollars," boomed the auctioneer. "The gentleman bids forty dollars. An *Alice* first, and I'm bid only forty dollars! Who'll make it forty-five; do I hear the five? *Shame*, ladies and gentlemen! Forty dollars once. Forty dollars once. Forty twice. Forty twice. Fair warning. Forty twice. Fair warning. Sold for forty dollars to Mr. Ellery Queen." He handed the book to an assistant, who placed it with the stacks of other volumes on the enormous library table.

Ellery added forty dollars to the total in his notebook. He had spent $3,895 in the last two hours, having bid in all volumes offered for sale, and had earned the eternal hatred of everyone in the library, except that of the auctioneer. At first the others had turned to look at him curiously when he outbid all competitors. But now only the gray-haired woman who had bid five dollars for the *Alice* and then dropped out shriveled him through her lorgnette. Most of the twoscore people in the room were either collectors or dealers. They were waiting impatiently, Ellery surmised, until the wild man's funds should be exhausted. Occasionally they would bid up the price of some volume to hurry the process.

The auctioneer, a round-faced, plump little man, who was posted on the notice as Rufus Smith, next sold several sets of standard authors in fine morocco. Ellery's total was increased to $4,222. The sets were left on the shelves, the assistants having written "E. Queen" on slips of paper and inserted one in the first volume of each set.

At four o'clock Mr. Smith announced that "the priceless items of the collection" would now be auctioned. Footing the column, Ellery saw that his purchases came to $12,567. Scarcely a dent in $250,000! The auctioneer swallowed half a glass of water and climbed to the second step of the library ladder that was used to reach the higher shelves.

"Ladies and gentlemen," he announced impressively, "I now have the rare privilege of offering you the only extant copy of the 1562 edition of Nostradamus's *Centuries*. The book alone is worth a fortune. But what places it in the category of the absolutely priceless books of the world is the inscription on the flyleaf." He opened the book and after a dramatic pause held it up for his audience to see. "Ladies and gentlemen, the inscription on this page is in the author's own hand, dedicating the work to Catherine de' Medici, the sixteenth century queen of France who instigated the Massacre of St. Bartholomew. It is dated 'le 14 avril 1562.' Who will open the bidding at $20,000?"

After a pause, someone behind Ellery nodded.

"Thank you, sir," said Smith. "I am bid twenty thousand. Do I hear twenty-five?"

"Twenty-one," Ellery said in a bored voice.

"Twenty-five," said the voice behind him.

Ellery glanced over his shoulder. To his surprise he saw Nikki Porter, his secretary, standing in the doorway. She was peering about the room, apparently looking for him. As he turned she spied him and started down the aisle. She looked worried about something, Ellery thought as she came towards him. He also thought her new permanent, bordering the green chapeau, was becoming.

"Twenty-six thousand," he said, with a polite yawn, and moved over to the next chair to make room for Nikki.

Nikki was not merely worried; she was in a funk.

At first, when she read Ellery's note, she had thought it was an attempt at humor; but as the afternoon passed and he did not return she began to wonder. She had read about the sale in the morning paper. She retrieved the *Times* from the scrapbasket and read the article again, making a note of the address of the Garten residence. At three o'clock she telephoned to Inspector Queen at police headquarters. He knew nothing about

Ellery's plans, but suggested without distress that Ellery might be a "little balmy." If he talked of spending $250,000 for books he undoubtedly was "completely cracked." He doubted if Ellery had more than $250 in the bank. Perhaps he'd added three ciphers by mistake instead of two for no cents.

Nikki had looked at the note again. Very definitely it said $250,000. Could Ellery have been drinking? Ellery —tight?

At three-thirty Nikki found that she was no longer able to keep her mind on her work. She was making one mistake after another. She could think of nothing but that strange note. Of course, his father had only been joking, but people did have nervous breakdowns, and Ellery *had* been overworking. Writing, writing, writing, as much as ten and twelve hours a day. And going without luncheon or sipping a mere cup of coffee from the cardboard container the corner drugstore sent it up in.

Well, if she couldn't work she might as well go over to the sale and see if he was being funny or—

Nikki dropped feebly onto the chair beside Ellery.

"Thirty thousand," said the voice behind Ellery.

"Thirty-one." Glancing down, Ellery saw that Nikki

was pale. Probably the permanent had been a strain. What women go through!

"Thirty-five thousand."

"Thirty-six," said Ellery, smiling at Nikki.

Nikki was shaking. Must pull herself together. Must get him out of here somehow.

The voice behind Ellery was silent—an irritated silence.

"Thirty-six I'm bid. Thirty-six once," Mr. Smith intoned. "Thirty-six once."

"Forty thousand." The voice had a waspish overtone.

"Forty-one," Ellery said apologetically. He was worried now. Something must have happened. Nikki looked as though she were going to be sick.

"Ellery," she whispered, "we've got to get out of here."

Why did she look at him with such big eyes, he wondered.

"What's wrong, Nikki?"

"Forty-five," said a beggarly-looking man in the front row. The dark horse. There is always a dark horse.

"Forty-five, forty-five, forty-five. Forty—"

"Six," said Ellery.

"Come on, Ellery. Please."

"I can't now. Tell me what's wrong, Nikki?"

"Forty-six thousand five hundred."

"Forty-six and a half. Who'll make it forty-seven?"

Ellery held up his hand. Nikki jerked it down.

"We've got to get out," she whispered. "Please, *please*."

"Mr. Queen bids forty-seven. Thank you, Mr. Queen. Do I hear forty-eight? Forty-seven thousand once. Forty-seven once. Twice. Fair warning. Forty-seven twice. Have you finished bidding? Fair warning! Sold to Mr. Queen for $47,000. I congratulate you, Mr. Queen."

"Will you tell me what's the matter, Nikki?"

"Nothing. Absolutely nothing, Ellery. Nothing's the matter," she said soothingly, as though she were speaking to a child. "Only please let's go." Her large brown eyes were frightened.

"I tell you I can't go," Ellery said testily. "If nothing's the matter, be quiet."

"Ladies and gentlemen, I now offer you a first edition of Francis Bacon's *Novum Organum*, published in 1620. Who will open the bidding?"

"Five hundred," said a man at Ellery's right.

"Six," said Ellery. This was too easy.

"Seven!" shouted his neighbor. "Shut up, will you?"

"Eight," said Ellery. "I beg your pardon?"

"Ellery. Something *has* happened." Nikki had begun to shake again. "I can't tell you here. Please come."

"Eight I'm bid. Do I hear nine?"

"Nine."

"A thousand," said Ellery gently.

"Thousand once. Twice. A thousand dollars twice. Sold. Sold to Mr. Queen." The auctioneer gave Mr. Queen a puzzled look, shrugged, took a sip of water, and continued. "The next item to be offered is the original manuscript of *Walter Raleigh His Pilgrimage*. You will recall, ladies and gentlemen, that Sir Walter wrote the verses while imprisoned in the Tower of London. Moreover, Queen Elizabeth—"

Ellery had touched Nikki's hand and found it cold as the deep. He rose, interrupting the auctioneer.

"Mr. Smith," he said, "I should like to make an offer for all the remaining volumes in the Garten Collection. I am willing to pay the price at which they are appraised in the catalogue. As I propose to bid in every item as it is offered, my purchasing the balance of the books for the figures mentioned will save everyone's time and preserve all our savoir-faire."

Feet moved, eyes popped, complexions rose.

The auctioneer cleared his throat. "Mr. Queen, that is

a matter I shall have to consult Mr. Garten about." He scuttled down the steps and disappeared through the doorway behind the ladder.

To Ellery's astonishment, Nikki had jumped up and was hurrying down the aisle between the rows of chairs. She disappeared after the auctioneer.

What in the world was the matter with the girl? She certainly was upset about something! Couldn't she see that he was doing his best to bring an end to the sale so that he could go with her? Couldn't she wait even a minute or two? Dashing off without a word of explanation! Probably all she had on her mind was that the hairdresser had cut her hair too short. Ah, females! She'd be all right in the morning. Nikki was quite wonderful of a morning.

Ellery became conscious of the fact that the people in the room were in a perilous mass mood. Several were leaving. The gray-haired lady practically spat at him as she passed. A trio on the opposite side of the room had their heads together, apparently plotting a lynching.

Ellery chuckled, looking comfortably out the window. The Garten house was the last on the street, and to the east he could see Welfare Island across the river. The house directly south, beyond the wood fence, was

John Mathews's residence. It was so close that Ellery could see Walter's uncle in a ground-floor library. The chair Mathews occupied stood near a closed window at the extreme right. An adjacent window was wide open, as was the French window, whose doors gave onto the garden terrace. A sudden movement at a window on the second floor attracted Ellery's attention. Shades of Poe! An enormous chimpanzee squatted on the windowsill. It was staring with complete absorption at its stomach while its long fingers explored for a flea. A woman with flaming red hair appeared and joined in the search. After a moment the chimp affectionately put his arm around her neck.

The woman, Ellery decided, must be Walter's maiden aunt, Carlotta Emerson. Walter always spoke of her as Aunty Carlo. Not much affection lost between them, or so—

"Mr. Queen."

Ellery saw Rufus Smith standing in the doorway, beckoning.

"Would you mind stepping in here a moment, Mr. Queen?"

The room proved to be Raymond Garten's study. Garten was a man of about fifty-five. The gray pouches beneath his eyes were made grayer by the shadow of his dark glasses. Wearing a house jacket of maroon velvet, he sat in a big leather chair, with a copy of the inventory on his lap. At a table near the middle of the room a man who appeared to be about Garten's age was adding columns of figures on a memorandum pad. Gray-haired, pale, hollow-chested, he might have been a caricature of an absent-minded professor. Beside him, to Ellery's annoyance, stood Nikki Porter, her usually wriggly little scarlet mouth set in a line that suggested Thermopylae, and "Remember the Maine," and things like that.

Mr. Garten got up and extended his hand towards Ellery.

"Mr. Queen," he said with a friendly smile, "although I've devoted my life to reading and collecting books"—he hesitated—"books of possibly greater—oh—depth than the ones you write, I want you to know that I'm an incurable Queen fan." He turned to the man at the table and said, "Henry, shake hands with Mr. Ellery Queen. Mr. Griswold is my librarian."

Henry Griswold looked up from his figures. He looked a little frightened.

"Yes, yes," he said, nervously. "If you don't mind my

saying so, you're much younger than I imagined you, and taller. You must be over six feet. Sorry to hear about your recent illness. One would never guess it to look at you."

"Illness?" Ellery blinked. He had not been ill a day in his life. Of course, he'd been beaten over the head and slugged several times. And there was that old bullet wound. . . . "I don't seem to recall being ill," he said politely. "Who's maligning me?"

The auctioneer coughed.

"This young lady—Miss Porter, I believe," he said, gesturing towards Nikki, "informs us that you have been ill—*are* ill, as a matter of fact."

Ellery frowned at Nikki.

"Is that so, Nikki? I didn't succumb, did I? You haven't sent the obituary notices to the papers, have you?"

"Oh, Ellery, that's just it. Of course you don't know. They never do. Please don't get excited. You've had a nervous breakdown. You've been working too hard. You'll be all right, Ellery. Really you will. You must rest and not get excited. You'll be all right again in no time," said Nikki breathlessly.

"Look here, Nikki, what have you been up to?" Ellery scowled. "Have you lost your mind?"

Again Rufus Smith coughed a little dry cough.

"The implication, sir, is that *you*—temporarily, of course, you understand, have — are — well, to put it bluntly—"

Griswold and Garten exchanged glances.

"Mr. Queen," the auctioneer began again as, speechless, Ellery stared at him, "you must understand that, in the circumstances, we don't want to do anything that will disquiet you. There will be no charges brought against you, or anything of the sort—although it is a serious offense to bid when one has insufficient assets to make good one's offer."

"Do you realize, Mr. Smith," Ellery asked gently, "that what you are saying is slander, defamation of character?"

Smith stepped backward, glancing at Nikki Porter for support.

"Ellery, you know you really haven't all that money," she said coaxingly, taking his arm. "Try to remember, Ellery. Please come. Everything will be all right. Please come now."

Ellery Queen grinned, but then he looked very stern.

"Mr. Smith," he asked coldly, "are you doing business with me, or with Miss Porter?"

"Why—why—" Smith mopped the back of his neck.

"My offer still holds," Ellery said, turning to Mr. Garten. "My bank, of course, is closed, but Mr. Jameson, the vice-president, usually stays until five o'clock. If you'll be good enough to call him—Midtown National—he'll assure you that my check up to a quarter of a million dollars will be honored. The number is Bryant 2-6200."

Garten hesitated. Then, with an embarrassed air, he dialed the number on the phone standing on a low table beside his chair.

"Oh, Ellery, Ellery!" Nikki leaned against the back of Griswold's chair, biting her lip.

"Is this the Midtown National? . . . Mr. Jameson, please. Hello! Mr. Jameson?"

Nikki was digging her fingers into the back of the chair. Somehow she had to keep from crying—from becoming hysterical. Poor Ellery. Oh, poor Ellery.

"This is Raymond Garten, Mr. Jameson. Mr. Ellery Queen has referred me to you. He says that you will verify that his check up to $250,000 will be honored by your bank on presentation."

After a while Garten said "Thank you" and replaced the receiver. He looked up at Ellery.

"Mr. Queen, we all owe you an apology." He turned towards Nikki Porter. "If this young lady—" he began, and stopped.

Nikki had fainted in Mr. Queen's arms.

CHAPTER III

THE VOICE OF DEATH

MR. ELLERY QUEEN kept close watch on the van ahead of his taxi as they drove up First Avenue. More than two hundred thousand dollars' worth of merchandise, whether books or gold bullion, might have an irresistible appeal to hijackers.

Nikki, thank Heaven, had come out of her faint a wiser woman. Wide-eyed she had listened on the sidewalk before the Garten residence to his account of Walter Mathews's visit, of John Mathews's fraudulent operations, of Walter's engagement to Marian, and Walter's quixotic desire to make restitution for the ruin his uncle had brought to Marian's father.

"Oh, Ellery, I'm so ashamed," she had begun and

then burst into tears. But when he asked if she had finished the typing he'd left for her, her tears stopped miraculously and she had exclaimed that of course she hadn't. She'd been too *worried*!

Ellery had promptly put her into a cab and sent her back to the office.

"Well," Ellery told himself, as the taxi followed the van through the underpass below the Queensboro Bridge, "a few more blocks and the Garten Collection will be out of my charge for good. Good!"

Through the haze that had descended on the late September evening came the vibrant note of the Welfare Island ferry making its way across the strong current to the slip on the opposite shore. The van turned west in the lower Eighties, the taxi swinging round the corner on its tail lights. After crossing Third Avenue, the driver pulled up to the curb behind the van. Ellery paid his fare and got out.

From the entrance of a yellow-brick apartment house Walter Mathews rushed to greet him.

"Are all the books—everything—in the van?" he demanded. "The works?"

"Every last book," Ellery said, "including three of Ellery Queen. Made me quite proud. Distinguished company. They were in a carton of miscellaneous rubbish that I bid in for seventy-five cents."

Walter slapped him on the shoulder exuberantly. "I've got the rooms ready. Hope we can get them all in. You bought the bookcases, didn't you?"

Ellery nodded.

"Had them thrown in. They're all there in the van—and four men to unload. They reached the Garten house about four-thirty, and we've made record time."

"Better than I even hoped. Marian ought to be here soon. I just phoned her. It's only five after five now. Did you see her?"

"I caught a glimpse of her. She barged in when the commotion started after Nikki tried to railroad me into an insane asylum."

"What do you mean? Was Nikki Porter at the sale?"

"Positively dominated it. Tell you about it later. Meanwhile—*en avant!*"

In the dingy lobby of the building Walter stopped to speak to Caesar Jones, the Negro at the switchboard. In addition to his job as telephone operator, Caesar ran the elevator. Walter's two-dollar tip persuaded him that it was quite all right for him to neglect the former duty in favor of the latter until the books had been deposited in the Gartens' third-floor apartment. Seeing the color of money, the moving men became enthusiastic. In fifteen minutes the Garten Collection was installed in the living room, dining room, and along three walls of the bedroom that Henry Griswold, Garten's librarian, was occupying. Walter had to admit that lining the wall behind the bed with books from floor to ceiling gave the room a learned if somewhat stoop-shouldered appearance. "Old Grissy will love it. He's as hopped about them as Mr. Garten is."

The van was just leaving when, impatient to hear the explanation of Walter's mysterious phone call, Marian Garten arrived with Griswold. Their surprise at first left them speechless. Wide-eyed, Marian stared at the books, at the grinning Walter, at Ellery Queen, and back at Walter again.

Ellery began to understand Walter's enthusiasm for yellow-haired, dark-eyed Marian. When she had come into Mr. Garten's study he had been too occupied with reviving Nikki to pay attention to another female. Now he saw that she was extraordinarily pretty. Twenty-one, he decided, with a figure of harmonious curves. But trim—as trim as Nikki's. Of course, Nikki's hair was nicer. Nikki's hair was golden brown, the color of autumn leaves. Marian Garten's was wheaty. But nice. Very.

"But I don't understand," Marian gasped.

Walter explained while Griswold went delightedly from case to case.

"Oh, *Walter*. How in the world will you get Father to accept them?"

"I don't have to. They're yours," Walter grinned. "He can't very well throw *your* books out of the place."

Marian looked worried.

"It's a miracle," Griswold chortled. "A miracle! We must break this gently to your father, Marian. The shock— You don't understand—any of you—what this will mean to him. His whole life— How we suffered while the auction—"

"Why isn't he with you gals and guys?" Walter demanded.

"He had something to attend to, darling," said Marian. "And when you phoned I couldn't understand what you were doing here. You sounded so excited. So I just got into a taxi. How *did* you get in, Walter?"

"I borrowed the key from your purse last night."

Marian laughed. "Pickpocket!"

No one paid attention to Ellery. Griswold was moving

along before the bookshelves. Occasionally he stroked a leather spine. When he came to the end of the row of cases, he paused and looked down at an envelope lying on a table.

Seeing him pick it up, Marian said, "It's from the bank. It came after you and Dad left this morning."

"I hope they're not pressing him," Griswold said, frowning, and then he smiled at Walter. "Of course, it's not so serious."

"Why don't you open it?" Marian suggested. "You've always handled Dad's business. If it's bad news it would be better not to tell him until he's had time to recover from the first shock. I won't be surprised if he tears up the check when he finds out that it is really Walter's money."

"Perhaps I had." Griswold slit the envelope open.

It contained, Ellery saw, a letter and what looked like a deposit slip.

Griswold studied both for several moments. Then he shook his head and stuffed the letter and envelope into his pocket.

"Is it all right?" Marian asked.

"Quite all right. Apparently the bank realized more than they anticipated from the sale of the securities."

He began once more to examine the spines of the books.

"Do you know what would make me completely happy now, Walter?" Marian asked. She turned to Ellery. "Mr. Queen, Walter's quarreled with his uncle—it's too silly—about something that's none of his business at all."

"Walter told me about it." Ellery smiled.

"Then don't you think they ought to make up? After all, Mr. Mathews has been like a father to him."

"I make it a point, Miss Garten, to give no advice on purely emotional issues."

"Won't you, please, Walter?" She slipped her arm through his. "For my sake?"

"Gosh, Marian, you know how I feel. And it's your father who's been hurt. How can you ask me to?"

"Don't you see if you're nice to your uncle you might get him to drill more test wells? It would be so wonderful if—"

"If that's what you're thinking about—" Walter began.

"But I'm not. It's not just that, really," she interrupted quickly. "If it hadn't been for me—Father, that is—you wouldn't have quarreled. You must see that that doesn't make me happy."

"What do you want me to do?" Walter asked impatiently. "Apologize for not liking his dirty work?"

"Darling, please! Honestly, Mr. Mathews thinks the world of you. Telephone him, and you'll see."

"Marian's right," Griswold said, looking up suddenly. "You ought to, Walter. You're finer than he is. Prove it."

He picked up his gray hat from the table. "I'll be back presently, my dear," he said to Marian. "I've got to get some preservatives for some of these leather books. I didn't bother to save any, thinking—"

"But you mustn't go now," Marian protested. "You must be here when Dad comes. Besides, it's too late. The stores will all be closed."

"Bloomingdale's is open until nine this evening," he said. "I'll be back before your father gets here. He was going to pack some of his personal things. You know how he putters about. I'll be back soon enough. Goodbye, Mr. Queen." He waved to Walter and hurried off.

As soon as the door closed behind Griswold, Marian turned once more to Walter.

"And now telephone your uncle," she said firmly.

Walter laughed.

"All right. See how love affects you, El?" He walked

resignedly over to the telephone and took off the receiver. After a moment he said, "Wire's open. Caesar's running the elevator—I can hear it, and the clock ticking on the switchboard. There—the elevator's down. Hello, Caesar? Get me Plaza 7-6202. . . . No, 6202."

"You're a lamb, Walter," Marian said, softly.

"Hello. Hello, Uncle John. Walter. . . . Yes, I'm at Marian's now. . . . What? . . . Oh! Well, yes. . . . Yes, I can come. . . . Decision? What about? . . . Oh, all right. I'll be there in ten, fifteen minutes." He hung up. "The old buzzard wants to see me."

"Didn't I *tell* you?"

"He didn't sound cordial. Sounded strange."

"How, strange?"

"Well, I don't know. Strange, that's all." Walter glanced at Ellery. "Look here, old man. Will you do me one last favor?"

"What?"

"I don't know how Mr. Garten's going to take this business about the books—my butting into his affairs. I wish you'd stay here with Marian until I get back. I won't be over half an hour. Then I'll blow you both to the best dinner in town. Champagne and a show after-

THE VOICE OF DEATH 37

wards. If Mr. Garten comes before I get back—well, if a stranger's present . . ."

Ellery looked at his watch. Five-thirty-five.

"But you two want to celebrate alone."

"There's always tomorrow! We'll get Nikki and have a foursome."

"And Walter's right about Father," Marian said. "You'll stay, won't you, Mr. Queen?"

Ellery threw up his hands. The day was killed, anyway. . . .

"Call Nikki right away," Walter said, grabbing his hat from one of the bookshelves. "See you all soon."

"Righto," Ellery said. "I'll call her—and if she's not at the office I'll wring her neck in the morning!"

Surprisingly, Nikki was still at the office. She'd be delighted! She'd work until seven, when they were to stop for her.

At six Marian excused herself, saying that she was going to slip into another dress and wouldn't be a minute. Ellery resigned himself to a long wait. But a few minutes later Marian came back, wearing an ice-blue frock that made her yellow hair shine like pale gold.

In similar circumstances, Nikki's "minute" would

mean anything from a half to three-quarters of an hour. Ellery glanced at his watch and congratulated Marian.

It was exactly six-seven—a fact which later he was to recall acutely, as did Marian when she learned that at precisely that moment Caesar Jones was looking at the clock on the switchboard and cursing the man who was supposed to relieve him at six and who was already seven minutes late.

Then, ten seconds later, Marian lifted the receiver and told Caesar to call Mr. Walter Mathews at Plaza 7-6202.

Within a half minute Caesar reported that the line was busy. But before she had a chance to hang up, he said, "All right, now, Miss Garten. Heah's Mistuh Mathews."

"Marian." Walter's voice was scarcely recognizable.

"What's the matter, Walter?"

Ellery watched the color slowly drain from Marian's cheeks.

"*Walter!* ... Yes, I'll tell him.... Yes, to hurry. Yes! Yes, right away!" She hung up, turned a stricken face on Ellery.

"Marian," said Ellery, gently, "what is it?"

Marian said in a choked voice: "He wants you to hurry down there. He kept saying for you to hurry. Walter's uncle—Mr. Mathews—has committed suicide."

CHAPTER IV

MURDER

THREE AUTOMOBILES, two of them police cars, were standing before the large stone residence of John Mathews when Ellery reached it. As he got out of his cab he saw that the third car was that of his father, Inspector Queen. He was halfway up the front steps when the plate-glass door, protected by an iron grille, was opened by a uniformed policeman stationed in the vestibule.

"Evening, Mr. Queen," he said. "The inspector said you'd probably be showing up. He's in the library. It's just back of the sitting room to your left."

Ellery Queen crossed the oak-paneled reception hall

and strolled through a formal drawing room. At the doorway to the library he paused.

The room was over thirty feet long, extending across the entire width of the house on the ground floor. The doors of the French window gave onto the terrace garden. It was these doors, still open, that he had seen during the afternoon from the Garten house in back of it. The window to the left of them also was open, he noticed. The three other windows were closed, as they had been earlier. On the floor, near a flat-top desk that faced the west wall of the room and about four feet from the closed window, lay the body of John Mathews. It was curled up, lying partly on the gray chenille rug and partly on the parquet floor, beside the desk chair that straddled the edge of the rug. Near his head the rug was stained a deep brownish-red. What caused the stain was gruesomely apparent. The nape of Mathews's neck was scarlet with blood. A few inches from his motionless left hand lay an automatic pistol. The position of the body suggested that he had been sitting in the chair when he shot himself and had toppled sideways from it to the floor.

In one of the two chintz-covered chairs by the fireplace at the other end of the room sat Walter, his face grim. Inspector Queen, a wiry little man with a gray moustache, Sergeant Velie towering at his side, stood gazing down at him.

"Oh, it's you, El," the inspector grunted. "Your young friend here has been telling me that he had a quarrel with his uncle. Immediately after, it seems, John Mathews shot himself. This youngster says he was with you from about five to five-thirty. Is that right?"

"I'd say so." Ellery stepped into the room. "I left the Garten house with the van of books at four-forty-five. It was five past five when I met Walter in front of the apartment house. He left there at five-thirty-five."

Ellery's presence seemed to reassure Walter. Almost immediately his face lost some of the strained look.

"You see, Inspector Queen," he said eagerly, rising, "I've been telling you the truth."

The inspector looked at him. "You got here a little before five-forty-five?"

Walter nodded.

"That's right. I noticed it was just five-forty-three by the clock in the reception hall."

"Who let you in?"

"Nobody. I let myself in with my key."

"Then there's no one to verify the time you got here?"

"Not that I know of—unless the taxi driver happened to notice."

"Make a note of that, Velie," the inspector ordered. "Try to locate the driver. He picked the cab up at Eighty-second and Second Avenue. Now about the ruckus." He turned back to Walter as the sergeant got out his notebook. "You admit—"

"Ellery," Walter interrupted, "I've told your father everything. About Uncle John's swindling Mr. Garten, about my clearing out, and about my engagement to Marian. When I talked with Uncle John on the phone, I told you he sounded queer. Well, he was. He acted queer when I got here. And I've admitted to Inspector Queen that we had a row this afternoon. Uncle John told me flatly that if I didn't come back immediately and give up Marian, he'd cut me out of his will. I told him plenty—exactly what sort of crook he was and that I wouldn't accept his dirty money if he left me fifty million—or whatever amount he'd swindled people out of during his lifetime."

"Fifty million bucks can stand an awful lot of dirt," Velie said dryly.

"I know what your father's thinking," Walter continued. "But you know, El, that I've got all the money I'll ever want. I despised Uncle John, I scrapped with him, but I didn't murder him. I wanted you to hurry over here, Ellery, so you could tell Inspector Queen that I'm telling the truth."

Ellery blinked.

"But I don't get the picture, Walter. What happened? Were you present when he shot himself?"

"No, I'd left."

"Then you came back? Why?"

"I heard the shot just as I was closing the front door. That is, I was in the vestibule. I ran back, and there he was, lying on the floor, shot."

"He shot himself—the instant you left?" Ellery stood motionless. "I'm trying to see this in temporal terms, Walter."

"Look," said Walter wearily. "After I told Uncle John what I thought of him, I went up to my room for my wrist watch. I'd forgotten it when I packed. I wasn't upstairs more than a moment. I just grabbed the watch and came back down. Then I went into the drawing room to get my hat. I chucked it onto the settee there when I got here. I glanced in here and saw Uncle John take out his pistol from the drawer where he kept it."

"Which drawer?" the inspector asked sharply.

"In that table between the windows." Walter pointed to a mahogany stand against the wall a few feet from where the body lay. "I was just about scared stiff. I thought he was going to kill me—I didn't know what to think. I wasn't armed, couldn't defend myself. . . . I ran like blazes. When I heard the shot, I stopped dead. I felt sick. Of course, I came back. He was dead, I guess. At least, he didn't move. I knew you were Ellery's father, Inspector, so I called you at once. Then I phoned Ellery at Marian Garten's."

"What time was that?" Inspector Queen asked.

"I don't know. I wasn't thinking of time."

"What time was it by your wrist watch when you got it from your room?" Ellery asked quickly.

"Can't say. It had run down. I didn't even stop to put it on. Here, look." Taking an oblong gold watch on a pigskin strap from the side pocket of his coat, he handed it to the inspector.

Inspector Queen verified the fact that it had run down. The hands pointed to eleven-seventeen.

"It was six minutes after six when he phoned headquarters, Inspector," Sergeant Thomas Velie said, rubbing his chin with one of his huge hands. His hands were in proportion to the rest of his enormous body. His thick, powerful fingers could easily have spanned six piano keys more than an octave.

Inspector Queen shot a glance at Velie. But before he could speak, animated voices rose from the reception hall. Someone was arguing loudly with the policeman who had been stationed in the vestibule. "Go see what the racket's about, Thomas," Inspector Queen said shortly. "Bring him in here, whoever it is." He turned back to Walter. "That's pretty thick—or thin, isn't it, Mathews? Am I to believe that your uncle killed himself because he was on the receiving end of a piece of his nephew's mind?"

Walter flushed.

"I didn't mean it that way, Inspector. I told him that I was going to get some of the stockholders to go to the district attorney and demand an investigation. He must have thought his goose was cooked—" He shrugged. "I don't know. I've told you everything I can."

Ellery studied Walter's face. It had become pale once more. Ellery was sure now he was not telling the whole truth. Only this morning he had admitted that the district attorney would be able to get nothing on John Mathews. Yet now he was suggesting that out of sheer funk his uncle had committed suicide. Why? It didn't check at all with the picture Walter had previously drawn of his uncle.

Velie had returned and was standing in the doorway with a big black-haired man wearing a handlebar moustache.

"Where's Mr. Mathews?" the man demanded gruffly, pointing the black derby hat in his hand at Walter.

Then he suddenly saw the answer to his question. His arm dropped; he gaped at the body. The derby slipped from his fingers. It described a half circle on the rug and came to rest against one of his highly polished shoes.

He turned quickly back to Walter.

"Walter! How'd this happen? What have you done? What—" He checked himself. "What's happened?" he said feebly. "Is—is he dead?"

"I'm Inspector Queen," the inspector said gruffly. "Your business with Mathews seems to have been urgent, judging from the way you were shouting in the hall just now. What's eating you?"

The big man shook his head slowly, as if to clear it. "I'm John Mathews's lawyer. He sent for me."

"Name?"

"Rhodes. Arthur F. Rhodes."

"When did Mathews send for you?"

"He telephoned my office a little after five-thirty—five-forty to be exact. Said he wanted to see me on a matter of great importance. I came as soon as I could. The officer at the door tried to stop me. Naturally, as Mr. Mathews's attorney, I resented his interference. I scarcely—"

"Why did you think a moment ago," the inspector demanded, "that Walter Mathews murdered his uncle?"

Rhodes stooped to pick up his hat.

"I thought nothing of the sort," he protested, puffing as though he were out of breath.

Inspector Queen watched Rhodes with his bright little eyes. "You burst in here and see John Mathews's body lying on the floor. You see the blood. You see the gun. Then you turn like a flash towards young Mathews and demand to know what he has done. It's too late now to cover up, Mr. Rhodes. Speak up!"

Rhodes scowled at the floor, then looked apologetically towards Walter.

"I'm sorry, Walter. But it's best to speak out now. The facts will come out sooner or later, anyhow. I'm just sorry that they have to come from me." He turned back to the inspector. "I asked that question impulsively," he said. "This morning Mr. Mathews telephoned me to cut Walter out of his will. He told me they had quarreled bitterly. When I came in—the shock, you know—my mind leaped to a conclusion automatically, to a completely false conclusion, doubtless. I have no doubt Walter's in no way responsible for—" He waved towards the opposite end of the room.

"Decent of you, Rhodes," Walter remarked. "I'd never have thought you liked me so much. Exactly what time did *you* leave here this afternoon?"

"What's this?" Inspector Queen demanded. "You were here earlier this afternoon, Mr. Rhodes?"

Rhodes's color deepened.

"I brought over Mr. Mathews's new will to be signed. I got here just after three o'clock. Lee will testify to that."

"Who's Lee?" the inspector asked.

"The Chinese servant. He let me in. I was here for only about ten minutes."

"Mr. Rhodes," Ellery said quietly, "was the will witnessed?"

"Naturally."

"By whom?"

"By Lee and my assistant, whom I brought along for that purpose."

"Did you and your assistant leave together?" Ellery lighted a cigarette and slipped the burnt match into his pocket.

"No. He left at once—as soon as he had witnessed Mr. Mathews's signature. I stayed a moment or two to talk over a confidential matter."

"Did anyone see you leave?"

"No one except Mr. Mathews. He walked to the door with me."

He looked at Ellery resentfully and then away. "Walter, has Miss Emerson been informed?"

Walter shook his head.

"She's my aunt," he explained, in answer to the inspector's questioning look. "She lives here. I didn't want to leave this room before you arrived."

"If you'll excuse me, Inspector," Rhodes said nervously, "I'll tell her at once. It will be a dreadful shock. She was very fond of John."

Inspector Queen nodded.

As Rhodes left the library, Dr. Prouty, the medical examiner, came briskly into the room, his hat perched on the back of his head. He plopped his small black satchel onto a chair, rolled the butt of a dead cigar from one corner of his mouth to the other, and stared coldly at his friend, Inspector Queen.

"Dick Queen," he growled, "I'm getting sick and tired of being sent for just when I'm starting for home! What is it now? Ah! Another stiff. Nothing but stiffs! Well, there'll be no autopsy tonight. Is that it, there? Or are you keeping another one from me as a surprise?"

"Good evening, Doc. Glad to see you in a better humor," Ellery said.

Prouty ignored him.

Inspector Queen said, "Oh, climb down, Prouty. Just got here a few minutes ago myself. Haven't had time to make any sort of examination. No one's touched the body. So don't fire *that* question at me." He motioned towards Walter. "This is Mr. Mathews, the nephew of the deceased. He found the body—says his uncle committed suicide. Young Mathews called us at six-six, immediately after he heard the shot. You'll notice the pistol is near the left hand. Mr. Mathews says his uncle was lefthanded."

"As if I cared!" said Prouty gaily. "Is the cadaver mine now? Or do I have to hang around watching you detect? Speak up, my old one!"

The inspector looked past the doctor towards the opposite end of the long room.

"Sic 'im, Fido," he said mildly. "And make a good job of it!"

Prouty snorted and picked up his bag.

A moment or two later, on his knees beside the body of John Mathews, he looked back over his shoulder.

"Suicide, did you say?" he demanded.

"That's what Walter Mathews said," Inspector Queen replied. "I told you the investigation's only just started."

"Suicide my foot," Prouty said. "Or yours. There's not a powder burn as big as a gnat's egg. This gent was murdered."

CHAPTER V

Miss Emerson

Dr. Prouty's announcement had a varied effect on the people in the Mathews library. Walter Mathews sank into the leather chair. The phlegmatic Velie merely grunted and crossed the room to watch the doctor continue his examination, beginning to look interested. Inspector Queen jumped for the telephone, giving orders an instant after he heard the word "murdered."

Ellery Queen's peculiar behavior brought Walter out of his trance. Ellery tossed his cigarette through the French window onto the lawn and, going to the doorway of the drawing room, stood for a moment with his back against the wall, close to an iron safe on his right.

Then he methodically took seven paces across the room once more to the threshold of the French window.

"Twenty feet wide," he muttered, and went into the drawing room.

Fascinated, Walter watched him pause at the settee. First Ellery looked down at the pearl-gray fedora hat that was lying on it; then he turned to look back into the library.

"Walter," he said, "did you kill Mathews?" He came back.

Walter blanched, but looked steadily into Ellery's eyes.

"No," he said. "I swear I didn't. That's why I sent for you. I knew I was in a spot. If you can't find out the truth I'll be sent to the chair. Ellery, you've got to help me!"

"When you get around to telling me the whole truth," Ellery drawled, "perhaps I will."

"But I've told the truth!"

Ellery shrugged.

"Suit yourself. What did you really go upstairs for after you left your uncle?"

"My wrist watch!"

"What else did you get?"

"Oh, I'd forgotten." Walter pulled a pair of suède

gloves from his side pocket. "When I opened the drawer to get the watch I saw these. I wear them when I drive, so I took them, too."

"What's this?" Inspector Queen had come up to Ellery and Walter. "What about the gloves?"

Walter explained.

The inspector blew through his straggly moustache. "So there'd be no fingerprints on the gun."

"No, sir." Walter jumped from the chair as though he had been jabbed with a pin. "I went up for the watch. I just happened to see the gloves, that's all."

Sergeant Velie joined the group.

"It's as clear as the nose on my face, Inspector," he announced. "Young Mathews here has a set-to with his uncle. His uncle cuts him out of his will. The young fellow goes up to get them gloves so his signature won't be on the gun. He goes to the table behind Mathews and gets the pistol. He's sitting beside the little table yonder when he shoots him." Velie pointed a formidable finger at the kidney table against the far wall and about ten feet from the desk chair beside which the body was lying.

"How do you know that he was sitting there?" Inspector Queen asked.

"Because Mathews was sitting at the flat-top desk

and he was shot in the neck. Doc says the bullet passed from right to left at a slight angle, and the guy that did the shooting was at least twelve feet away, because there ain't no powder marks. Then he sets the gun down near the hand so it'll look like suicide and calls the police."

"Sounds reasonable, Thomas," Inspector Queen said thoughtfully. "But I don't know about some of your details. How do we know that Mathews was sitting in the desk chair, for instance?"

"That's easy," the sergeant said confidently. "The bullet went out the window. It's not in the room and not in the neck, so it must of. Now if he was standing, then the bullet would of busted a pane in the upper part of the window or would of gone into the wall. Only it didn't. Because I've looked, and it didn't." The sergeant went into the library, sat beside the kidney table, and squinted past the desk chair out the open window. Returning, he said, "If it wasn't deflected, it must of landed in the East River. It wouldn't carry clear over to Welfare Island after going through his backbone. The doc says it splintered the third something to bits—in the neck, I mean."

"Well, Mathews," the inspector said, "you hear what

Sergeant Velie says. You must realize that under the circumstances—"

"Just a minute, Dad," Ellery interrupted. "Before you hold Walter on suspicion of murder, I'd like a couple of words with you in private. As a favor to me, will you hold off awhile? You can keep him under arrest in his room, at least while you're questioning the other members of the household."

"Son," the inspector said, scowling, "that's just what I was planning to do. I wish you'd remember I was investigating crimes when you were playing Red Rover." He stopped abruptly on seeing Dr. Prouty, satchel in hand, slouching towards the door. "Hey, Prouty, where do you think you're going?"

In the doorway Prouty said quickly, "I left my report on the desk."

"You'll have to do a p.m. tonight," the inspector said with enjoyment.

Prouty hesitated.

As soon as Walter, escorted by Flint, a plainclothes man, had left for his room on the second floor, Inspector Queen turned to Ellery.

"Now what have you got on your mind, son?"

"Nothing vital, Dad. I just wanted to point out that

if you and Velie are swayed by circumstantial evidence you may overlook certain possibilities."

"I'm always ready to listen to reason, El. But you'll have to admit, if you face the facts, that your boyfriend hasn't a leg to stand on."

"That's precisely one of the points I was about to make. He's an intelligent kid with a quick mind. He would be intelligent enough, if he did murder his uncle, to try to make the death look like suicide. In his excitement he might forget about powder burns, I'll admit. But no one came running in here after the shot was fired. Apparently no one heard it or, if they did, paid no attention to it. Most people can't tell the difference between the sound of a car backfiring and a pistol shot. Now if Walter is guilty and no one came barging in on him, why would he be so completely dumb as to call the police? By doing so he fixes the exact time of the crime and proves his presence here at that time. If he'd simply left without notifying anybody, you'd have had a hard time proving the exact time of the murder or proving that he hadn't left before it was committed. Now why, I ask you, would Walter not clear out at once if he were guilty? Yes, there are lots of 'clever' answers possible—but you know how few crimes are solved by 'clever' answers!"

The inspector was not impressed.

"Man's reasoning powers don't function normally just after he's committed a murder," he said, "no matter how bright he was in school."

"Don't get me wrong," Ellery said quickly. "I'm not claiming that Walter's innocent. I'm just pointing out that the circumstances don't necessarily prove his guilt. From them you can reason just as logically that he's innocent. Besides, you haven't begun to consider the other possibilities."

"What other possibilities?"

"Walter says that he was standing by the settee in the drawing room when he saw Mathews take the pistol from the table drawer. From that position you can't see all of this room. You can see from a few feet to the right of the French window over to the leg of the desk chair the body's lying beside—the left back leg, that is—the one that's on the rug. Twenty people could have been in here without Walter's having seen them. He says he just took one look and ran. Anyone could have come in either through the drawing room or through the French window while he was upstairs."

"Mmm," said Inspector Queen. "You like Walter, and you're doing a little wishful thinking on his behalf." He patted Ellery's shoulder. "Don't blame you at all. Well! Guess I'll question the inmates here. What a life!"

The police photographer and fingerprint men arrived a few minutes later. They set to work immediately in the library. Inspector Queen instructed Velie to canvass the neighborhood, inquiring particularly if anyone had heard a pistol shot shortly after five o'clock. Closing the library door, he sent a plainclothes man whom he called Jimmy to ask Miss Emerson, Walter's aunt, to come down to the drawing room.

A few minutes later, accompanied by Rhodes, Miss Emerson, a full-blown woman in her late thirties or early forties, came into the room. The inspector introduced himself and Ellery.

"As I was sure it would be," Rhodes said ponderously, "Mr. Mathews's death has been a great shock to Miss Emerson. I trust that you won't unnecessarily tax her strength by questioning her at length just now."

"I'm not given to questioning people unnecessarily

at any time, Mr. Rhodes," the inspector said gently. "Won't you please sit down, Miss Emerson? Naturally, I want to offer my sympathy, and I'll be as brief as I can."

Nothing about Carlotta Emerson justified Rhodes's concern for her "strength." "Horsy" was Ellery's secret word for her. Her superb carriage, square shoulders, and strong hands for some reason made him think of her as a woman who spent hours daily on the bridle path. Because of her Amazonian appearance, which was accentuated by her gray tweed suit, her voice so astonished Ellery that he believed either his eyes or his ears must be deceiving him.

Instead of the deep, throaty tones he had expected, what he heard was more feminine than the affected baby-talk of a sixteen-year-old girl. Carlotta Emerson cooed and chirruped almost flirtatiously and spoke with an accent that resembled nothing he had ever heard off a vaudeville stage.

Miss Emerson's grandparents had been born in Richmond and, although she had never lived south of Philadelphia, she had cultivated for social purposes an accent that she believed to denote true genteel Virginia. This belief, alas, was not borne out by the result. Occasionally she forgot herself; it was then that New York shouldered itself rudely through the soft absurdities of her speech.

"Eu, no, Mistah Queen," she said in response to his question, after she had floated to rest on the settee. "Ah didn't heah Waltah when he arrived. Ah was having mah siesta. Though latah Ah heard them qua'ling."

"Did you hear what the quarrel was about?"

"Eu, no. Ah hate qua'ls, and they were always qua'ling. Ah got up and closed the window so Ah wouldn't heah. Besides, it excites Togo."

"Togo?"

"Yes, mah chimp. He's such a sensitive dah'lin'."

"Chimp?" Inspector Queen's bushy eyebrows rose.

"Yes. Mah chimpanzee." She folded her strong hands demurely.

"During the afternoon did you hear anything that sounded like a pistol shot?"

"Yes. But thah's been so much shootin' across the way that Ah thought nothin' of it."

"Shooting? How's that?" the inspector asked, straightening up in his chair.

"Eu, ouah neighbahs practice shootin' in their cellah,

and when they leave the cellah do'ah open you can heah the shots."

"Which neighbors?"

"The people in ouah reah. Mistah Gah'ten and his librarian."

"Oh," said Inspector Queen. "Did you hear more than one shot?"

"Only one."

"Do you know at what time you heard it?"

"It must have been about six or maybe just befoah. It was befoah six-five, Ah'm suhtain-suah."

"What makes you so sure, Miss Emerson?"

"Because it was several minutes latah that Ah heah'd the Boston boat."

"Do you mean you saw it—from the window?"

"No, Ah *heah'd* it. The whistle. It blows the whistle every evening when it passes heah at five minutes past six."

Ellery was suddenly tense. If what Carlotta had said was true, it was a damning bit of evidence against Walter. What had Walter been doing the five or more minutes after the shot was fired?"

Ellery Queen got up, slipped out of the room. In

the library he spoke to the man who was photographing fingerprints.

"Many?" Ellery asked.

"Loads of them—all over the place."

"Any clues?"

"Nothing to get excited about. We vacuumed the place. Maybe the lab will turn something up when they analyze the stuff in the cleaner. And then we found a funny-looking pin down between the upholstery of the chair over there."

"Which chair?"

"The one beside that dinky table."

"Where's the pin?"

"On the desk."

"Say, Mr. Queen," called a man who was packing up a large camera and other paraphernalia, "we're through with the job. They can take the stiff away now. Is it all right to go through the room the chief's questioning the bunch in?"

"You'd better knock and find out," Ellery mumbled.

By the light of the electric lamp on the desk he was examining the green quartz pin that lay on the desk. The stone was octagonal, about five-eighths of an inch in diameter, and set in gold. Mounted on the face of the stone, also in gold, were the Greek letters alpha, beta, gamma. It was obviously a fraternity pin. He turned it over and saw the legend, "R.G. 1909," chased on the back.

"R.G.—Raymond Garten," he murmured.

However, he did not need the evidence of the initials to inform him that the pin belonged to Marian's father. He had seen it pinned to the black waistcoat Garten had been wearing under his maroon house jacket that very afternoon.

Ellery automatically crossed to the French window and stared out at the back of the Garten residence. Lights shone from the windows of the house to the east of it. But the Garten house was ominously dark and forbidding, the roof etched against the sky that now glowed with the reflected lights of the city. Deep in thought, he did not hear the detectives leave the room.

"That," he concluded after a minute or two, "explains something. But it makes nine-tenths of it absolutely unexplainable."

A moment later he was on his hands and knees, creeping about the room like—he would not have been flattered by the simile—a large chimpanzee.

CHAPTER VI

Clues

WHEN ELLERY QUEEN returned to the drawing room he found his father questioning Lee, a fat Chinese valet, who said he had been in Mr. Mathews's employ for six years. At first Lee was exasperatingly uncommunicative, answering for the most part in monosyllables. But then he warmed up. According to the Chinese valet there were three pistols in the house. It seemed that Mr. Mathews had bought them after receiving threatening notes sent anonymously by investors in one of his companies.

"Sort of industrial fan letters," thought Ellery with a grin.

"Missa Mathews," Lee said, "give one pistol Missie

Emerson, one Missa Walter, one he keep self in library. He get license three pistol."

Lee confirmed what the other two servants had told the inspector. A couple, the wife a cook, the husband a butler, had been employed only two days before. The couple previously employed in the Mathews ménage had left in a huff when they learned that their savings had been lost. Mathews had not felt it necessary to make their losses good; he had not advised them to buy Chickawassi stock. They had invested their money on the strength of what the butler overheard at the dinner table.

Lee also confirmed Carlotta Emerson's testimony about the approximate time of the pistol shot. Each day he rested in his room on the third floor from five-thirty until suppertime. He always went down to the kitchen for his supper shortly after six, and he got up when he heard the steamboat's whistle. On the way down he would put a decanter of sherry and a glass in the library for Mr. Mathews. The whistle always blew at exactly the same time. He had checked it often by his clock. It had never been more than half a minute off. The shot had been fired five or ten minutes before he heard the whistle that afternoon. He was half asleep and at the time thought a car had backfired on the East River Drive. It had a muffled sound, and he thought it was from the uptown traffic, on the lower level of the concrete drive. It sounded to him as if it came from the lower level. But as his room was at the back of the house directly over the library, he now was ready to believe that what he had heard must have been the firing of a pistol in the library. Shown the pistol, he could not tell whether it was Mr. Mathews's or one of the others. They were all exactly alike.

"Now, Lee," the inspector asked, "you say you customarily stop in the library on your way to the kitchen? You do that invariably—every day, that is?"

"Yessa. Except when Missa Mathews have guest. Then mebbe he tell me make cocktail."

"You always go immediately to the library after you get up?"

"Yessa. No take clothes off to nap. Go down light away."

"And today, when you found Mr. Walter Mathews, what was he doing?"

"Telephone. Yessa."

"Do you know to whom?"

"Nosa."

"What was he saying?"

"He tell someone please hully."

"That's all you heard?"

"Yessa."

"You noticed nothing unusual?"

"I see Missa Mathews on floor. 'Assall."

"Then Mr. Walter told you to go to the kitchen and stay there until the police arrived?"

"Yessa."

"And that's what you did?"

"Yessa."

"That's all for now, Lee."

"Dad," Ellery said when the Chinese had left, "I've drawn a sketch of the library. If you'll take a look at it, I think you may change your entire angle of reasoning, especially about Walter."

The inspector's bushy eyebrows contracted.

"Hold your horses, son. I know what you're getting at. We have two witnesses who place the firing of the shot from five to ten minutes before the time Walter says he heard it. It's obvious that one of the two claims is false, and in my opinion the minority loses in this case."

Ellery nodded.

"I agree on that point. When I heard Miss Emerson tell her story, I felt sure Walter'd lied about the time, and I went over every square inch of the library to find out why he lied. My sketch gives the answer." He took a sheet of note paper from his pocket and handed it to his father.

Without even glancing at it, the inspector said, "I know why he lied, without any sketch of the room or other nonsense. You didn't hear what the cook or the butler had to say, El. If you'd stuck around and not wasted your time drawing pictures you'd know that Walter is as guilty as Old Nick. The butler went out the basement door at a few minutes before six for a breath of air, he says. He stood on the sidewalk directly in front of the house until he heard the whistle of the Boston boat. Then he went in, as he knew it was suppertime. Don't you see, that explains Walter's lie and his waiting for five or ten minutes after he'd killed Mathews before he phoned the police?"

Ellery smiled.

"No, I don't see," he said.

"Well, son, as a rule you're a little quicker." Inspector Queen chuckled, but his glance was sharp. "Walter Mathews was trapped, and he knew it. He'd gone upstairs to get his gloves. Having put them on, he took the gun from the table downstairs, stepped round to the kidney-shaped table, and shot his uncle, who was sitting in the chair. As Velie pointed out, shot from that angle, the bullet would go out the open window. Walter put the gun down near Mathews's hand so that the death would look like suicide and ran for the front door. But there was the butler right in front. He waits, hoping that Clarkson—that's the butler's name—will go back into the house. But apparently Clarkson was going to stand there indefinitely. Then the river whistle blows, and Walter realizes that in a minute Lee will come downstairs and go into the library with the sherry. He hurries back and telephones the police that Mathews has killed himself. It's the only possible escape he has."

"Why didn't he go out the back way?" Ellery asked, skeptically. "There's a passageway between this house and the one just west of it. Incidentally, anyone could have come into the house that way, since the French doors in the library stood open. Besides, there's another passage between the Garten house and the one next to it. If you argue that Clarkson would have seen him when he came out of the passage, then Walter could have climbed over the fence and come out on the street north of here."

"Fiddle-de-dee! The chances would be a thousand to one that someone'd see him scaling the fence. It was light enough for him to be recognized. It would have been practically a confession of guilt."

Ellery's forehead wrinkled.

"Dad, Raymond Garten was here this afternoon."

The inspector started.

"How do you know?"

"He was wearing this on his waistcoat," Ellery said, handing his father the pin, "at the auction sale earlier today. *But he lost it here.* It had slipped down under the cushion of the chair by the kidney table."

"Well, what of it?"

"Garten had a strong motive for wishing to blow John Mathews's brains out. Mathews had ruined him."

The inspector scowled.

"You mean Garten may have come over the fence, shot Mathews, and got caught in the act by Walter when he came down after getting the watch and gloves? But Walter's in love with Marian and hates his uncle, anyhow. So he waits, until Garten has had time to get away and establish an alibi, before calling the police. Is that the idea?"

"Expressed, Dad," murmured Ellery, "with laconic eloquence."

"It's possible." The inspector was thoughtfully examining the pin Ellery had handed him when Sergeant Velie came into the room.

"Well, Thomas?"

"I could find only two people who heard the shot, Chief. The chauffeur who works next door was in the kitchen at the back, chinning with the cook. He stuck his neck out the window when he heard it. But the cook told him not to get excited, that it was just the folks in the Garten house practicing again. He's only been on the job a week, so he didn't know about the basement shooting gallery."

"Did they hear it before or after six?"

"Funny you'd ask that, Chief. I can't figure it out, because the kitchen clock was right. I checked it. The chauf says it was just two minutes before six. He was supposed to be out in the car at six, so he was keeping an eye on the clock. He'd just picked up his cap to go out front when he heard the bang. Now if Walter Mathews—"

"Never mind that, Velie," Inspector Queen interrupted. "El has one notion and I've got another about why Walter waited before reporting to the police. A third would give me a headache! What else did the neighbors see or hear?"

"An old lady across the street saw a man that fits this Rhodes guy's description, handlebar moustache and all, come out of here a little after three."

"That's when he said he left. What of it?" the inspector barked.

"Nothing—his coming out, I mean. The interesting thing is that she saw him look up at a dame, Miss Emerson, I guess; she saw the dame had red hair—and then Rhodes went back up the steps and waited until she let him in the front door."

"This gets thicker by the minute." Inspector Queen worried his moustache. "How long did Rhodes stay?"

"The lady don't know. She went to make herself a cup of tea. Tea! She sits at the window every afternoon. She likes to watch the boats on the river . . . *she* says. Ol' snoop! But say, Chief—"

"Well, say it!"

"That chimp. I got an earful about the chimp from the super of one of the buildings on the block north. The building has a roof garden, and the super goes up there to look through a pair of binoculars when he

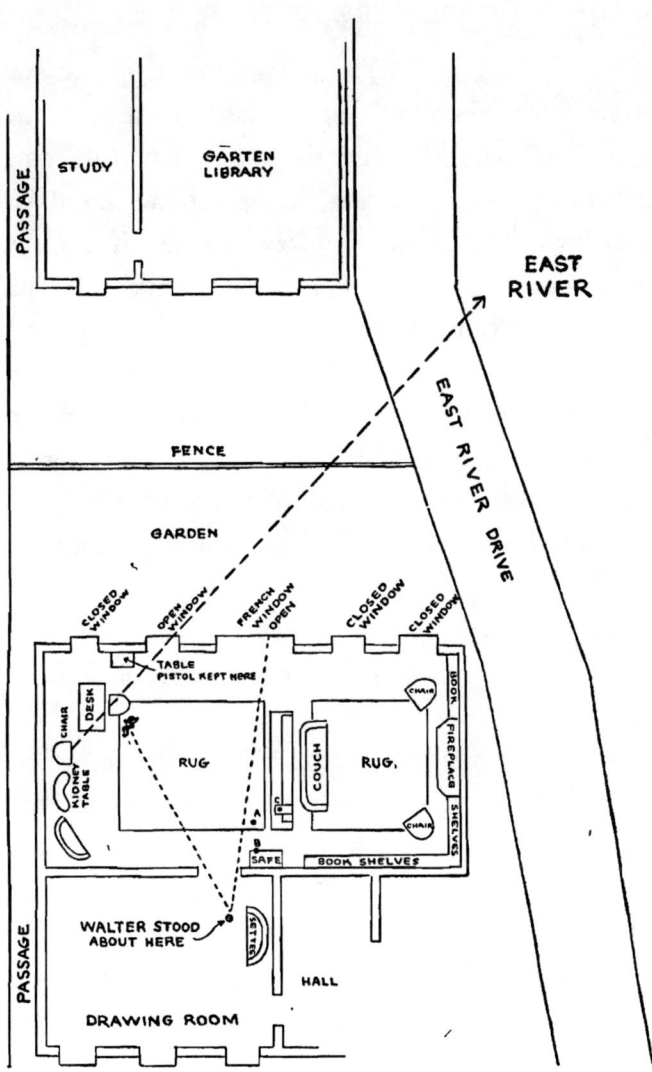

hasn't anything to do. Just for the fun of it, you see. Looks at the prison on Welfare Island and all over the place." Velie chuckled, "Maybe to look into a window or two, too! Well, he says that chimp can do about everything. The blasted monkey can eat off a plate, drink out of a cup. He's watched her—Miss Emerson, that is—train him. He even goes up the drainpipe and through her window and brings her her coat sometimes. Can you beat it? Another time the chimp climbed over into the Gartens' yard, swiped a watering pot, and scooted up to the roof of this house with it."

"What did it do there?" Ellery asked. "Water the roof?"

"The can was empty," said Velie, reddening.

"Just what has all this to do with the investigation?" Inspector Queen demanded softly.

"Well, I dunno." Velie looked hurt. "It just strikes me as a blamed queer sort of pet for a dame to have around the place. I think she's a phony."

The inspector turned away from his subordinate. He spread Ellery's sketch out on a table.

"Well, son, what is it about your pretty picture that's going to revolutionize my whole conception of the Mathews murder?" he asked ironically. "Please give me something more concrete than a member of the household's interest in pets."

Sulkily, Velie moved over and stood beside the inspector, surveying the sketch.

After examining the plan for a moment or two, Inspector Queen asked, "What are the dotted lines for, El?"

"They indicate the part of the library that can be seen from the settee, where Walter says he left his hat. The rest of the room would be outside his range of vision."

"What's the idea of the B on the corner of the safe?" Velie demanded.

"Paint's chipped off there. The safe's about three feet high. The mark is near the top."

"And C—what's that, son?"

"There are twenty books across the back of the table between marble bookends. The fifth volume from the end is sticking out about three inches beyond the others. It's Johnson's *Wills and Testaments*."

"And the funny-lookin' thing beside the desk chair marked X—is that supposed to be the body?" Velie seemed to be amused.

"No. That's the bloodstain on the rug. The dot by

the A represents a depression in the rug. The body isn't in the picture."

"Depression? What do you mean, son?"

"The nap of the chenille is pressed down."

"Proving that the murderer was lame and had a crutch, I suppose," Velie said sarcastically. "Say, that broken line, Mr. Queen, that's the flight of the bullet, all right. That's what I told you. It landed in the river."

"Well, El," said the inspector, "my mind doesn't seem to have done any flipflops. We'll look into the Raymond Garten angle, of course. That makes sense. But if I were you, son, I'd stick to writing and not try to go in for art. Here's your sketch." He handed the paper back to Ellery.

Ellery smiled again. "Don't say I didn't warn you!"

He stopped short as they all turned to stare at the doorway to the hall. Someone was thumping down the stairs, apparently three at a time.

A moment later, Flint, the plainclothes man who had been assigned to guard Walter Mathews, burst into the room.

"Say, Chief," he roared angrily, "young Mathews did a fade. Took a powder! Fooled me, blast him! He got out the bathroom window."

CHAPTER VII

Money Talks

Two minutes after Detective Flint's announcement, orders for the apprehension of Walter Mathews were being broadcast over the police short-wave and teletype systems.

Flint's angry confession was brief. Walter had fooled him with one of the oldest tricks in the criminal records. He had asked for permission to go to the bathroom. The detective had escorted him there and had stood in the hall by the door. After a few minutes he had knocked and, receiving no reply, had forced the lock. Walter had apparently lowered himself from the window ledge and dropped from the second floor into the passageway between the buildings.

Inspector Queen's orders were even briefer than Flint's explanation. He sent Flint back to headquarters after exactly five seconds of cold glare, at which Flint turned pale. Then, leaving Sergeant Velie on guard in the library, the inspector went with Ellery to Walter's room.

They found that Walter had left none of his personal belongings. Everything had apparently been removed previously to the Yale Club. The gun that his uncle had given him, the chief object of the inspector's search, was nowhere to be found. Lee was sent for. He said positively that he had seen it in the top drawer of the bureau the day before. Missa Walter must, he insisted, have packed it up with his other things.

Dismissing Lee, the inspector crossed the hall and knocked on Miss Emerson's door. Apparently she had been listening at it, for Ellery heard her rush away from it and then walk back to it.

"Eu, Mistah Queen," she said as she opened the door.

"I understand that Mr. Mathews gave you a pistol some time ago," the inspector said. "Mind if we come in?"

"Do, Inspectah." She swung the door wide open and

stepped back. "Yes, John was nervous about some lettuhs he received."

"Do you know if he kept the letters?" Ellery asked, following his father into the room.

"Nooo— Ah reahly don't know. He didn't show them to me."

"Where do you keep the pistol?" the inspector asked.

"In the drawer beside my bed."

"Will you get it for me, please?"

"Eu, of co'se, Inspectah," she said, crossing the room. "Ah reahly thought it was very silly; and Ah don't think pistols—not loaded ones—should be left lying around. Not that— Why! Why!" She had pulled open the drawer of the stand beside her bed. "Eu! Mistah Queen! It's not there. It's gone!"

Inspector Queen went to her side and looked down. Except for a small book entitled *Courtship and Marriage*, the drawer was empty.

"When did you last see it there?" he demanded.

"Ah don't think Ah've opened the drawer since Ah put the pistol theah. What could have become of it?" She clapped her hand over her mouth and stared wide-eyed at Inspector Queen. "You don't think—" she whispered through her fingers. "You don't think that he—the pistol—that he took it?"

"Who?"

"John. Why!—That Mr. Mathews killed—"

"When did you put the pistol in this drawer, Miss Emerson?"

"The day he gave it to me."

"But when was that?" the inspector asked impatiently.

"Last Wednesday—when he came home in the evening." She sank down on the edge of the bed, stroking its cover of lavender taffeta as she stared, horrified, at the drawer.

At nine o'clock, having left Sergeant Velie in charge at the Mathews residence, the inspector and Ellery drove to Raymond Garten's new and modest apartment, stopping on the way for a hasty supper in a lunchroom on First Avenue.

Marian Garten opened the door in response to their ring; she was still wearing the blue dress. She was momentarily startled when Ellery introduced his father as Inspector Queen, but she recovered immediately and asked Ellery about the tragedy and about Walter. He answered her evasively, saying only that Walter had been too upset by his uncle's death to talk with anyone. No doubt he would call her later that evening or in the morning.

"This is dreadful news about John Mathews," Mr. Garten said when they all went into the living room. "I can't understand his doing such a thing. Can't understand it at all."

Henry Griswold was unmoved by Mathews's death. After nodding to the inspector in acknowledgment of the introduction, he continued to rub something that looked like brown salve into the leather binding of a book. "Served him bloody right," Ellery heard him mutter. "Suicide! Conscience! Only decent thing he ever did."

"I see that you got your preservative, Mr. Griswold," Ellery remarked.

"Eh? Oh! As a matter of fact, I didn't," Griswold answered, continuing to massage the book. "They were all out of it. Had to get saddle soap instead—from the shoe department!" he added disgustedly. "So Mathews blew his brains out, did he? It's no great loss to the world."

"Mr. Garten," Inspector Queen said, "I understand

that you called on John Mathews this afternoon."

"Yes. Yes, I did." Garten looked sharply at the inspector. "That's why I can't understand this at all. It's the last thing in the world I should have expected."

"How do you mean?"

"Why—" Garten hesitated. "Why, he was thoroughly pleased with himself when I talked with him. Not at all like a man who was intending to take his own life."

"When were you at his house?"

Garten thought for a moment. "I think it must have been around five-fifteen." He turned to Marian. "What time did you and Henry leave the house, Marian?"

"At five-ten." Griswold answered for her.

"That's right," she agreed. "Walter phoned me shortly after five, and we left almost at once."

"Well," Garten said, "then it was about five-fifteen when I went round to see John, for I just put a few more odds and ends in my bags and then went on over." He nodded at two suitcases that stood beside the doorway to the hall. "There doesn't seem to be any end to it. Every time I go down to the house I bring back another load."

"How long were you with Mathews?" the inspector asked.

"About ten minutes."

"Then what did you do—after you left him?"

Garten wrinkled his forehead.

"Why are you asking me these questions, Inspector Queen? Is something—anything—"

"There's always a routine checkup in cases of suicide," the inspector said pleasantly. "Of course you don't have to answer, but it will make things easier for me if you do."

"Oh, gladly, gladly. As a matter of fact, I went for a walk to cool off. I was very angry, angry and depressed—depressed because I thought I'd lost my library for good. I never dreamed that Walter would do such a fantastically generous thing. I suppose your son has told you, Inspector?

"I was angry at John Mathews," he continued without waiting for an answer. "Furious! I didn't want Marian to know how upset I was. She always worries so about me. So I stayed away until I'd cooled off. Then I went back to the house, got my bags, and came here in a taxi."

"And at what time did you get home?"

"Home? Oh, you mean *here*. What time was it, dear, when I came in?" he asked Marian.

"Just after six-thirty." Marian did not take her gaze from the inspector's face. She had been watching him intently from the moment he had sat down opposite her father.

"That's about right," Griswold agreed. "I got back from Bloomingdale's about ten minutes before you came in, Raymond."

"It would take you about ten minutes to drive from your former home here, wouldn't it, Mr. Garten?"

"Possibly a little less," Garten said, pursing his lips.

"Then you must have left there about six-twenty. Were you in the house long?"

"No. I left the bags in the hall before I went over to see Mathews. I just picked them up and put them in the taxi. I'd driven over in the taxi from Second Avenue. It was waiting in front."

"Do you mind telling me, please, why you were angry at Mr. Mathews?"

"I suppose you've heard, Inspector," Garten said grimly, "that John Mathews was responsible for my financial losses—not only mine but those of a good many of my friends." He glanced across the room at the librarian and then turned back to Inspector Queen. "Well, I decided that Walter was right—that John

Mathews should be forced to go on drilling for oil on the property. I went to make him one last appeal. Heaven only knows how many millions he'd made out of the deal. I told him that he could easily afford to put up half a million to rehabilitate the corporation and that in the name of common decency he ought to do it. He just laughed at me. Then I told him that I was going to the district attorney to demand an investigation."

"How did he react to that?" Inspector Queen asked.

"In a way that surprised me out of my senses. He came over and patted me on the back in the most friendly way."

"Where were you sitting, Mr. Garten?" Ellery asked.

Garten blinked at him.

"Why, let me see—I was sitting beside that little table—the kidney-shaped table. Mathews had been sitting at his desk near the window. He just patted my back and went back again and sat down. At first I couldn't understand what he was talking about. Gradually the whole outrageous business dawned on me. You see, in the most natural sort of way he pretended that I'd known all along that the whole scheme was crooked. He told me not to worry about any stockholders going to the D.A. because the D.A. couldn't get anything on *us*. When he said 'us' I could have fallen out of the chair. I couldn't imagine what he was talking about." He paused and sat for a moment frowning down at the rug.

Griswold had stopped rubbing saddle soap on the leather book and, with a puzzled look, was watching Garten.

"Mathews saw that I was bewildered and laughed again," Garten continued. " 'Raymond,' he said, 'cut out the play-acting. You've got your cut in the profits. Why put on this act? All you have to do is to lie low for a year and then tell your friends that you've recouped on the stock market. Be your age.' Still bewildered, I asked what he was talking about. Then he changed his tone and said seriously, 'Ray, you put $150,000 into Chickawassi, right?' I nodded. 'Well, yesterday I deposited $200,000 in your account at your bank. So I wouldn't be in a hurry to go to the D.A. if I were you. When it gets out that you made a cool $50,000 on the deal, one of your "friends" is apt to blow your head off. There are certain things nobody can explain away, Ray, so if I were you I'd just keep my mouth shut.'

"Well, Inspector, now you can understand why I wanted to be alone for a while to cool off and to think the thing out. I finally decided that the thing to do was to go down to the bank in the morning, tell the man I do business with there all about the situation, and have him send a cashier's check for the $200,000 to Mathews. Then at least I would have had a clear conscience. I wasn't going to mention the matter to anyone except to Mr. Griswold here. Mathews was right. There are certain things you can't make people believe. He'd shut my mouth, just as he told me he had. But now his suicide complicates matters. Of course, I'll send the check to his estate, and pray Heaven no one ever hears about it. The bank wouldn't have to disclose who bought the cashier's check unless the court ordered it to—and that's not likely."

"Mathews appears to have been a very clever galoot," Ellery Queen said and, getting up suddenly, crossed to the doorway. "Do you mind, Mr. Garten, if I peep into your suitcase?"

Garten bristled. "Why, why should you want to do an extraordinary thing like that, Mr. Queen?" he asked stiffly.

"Is there any reason why you should refuse?"

"If you put it that way, none besides a natural dislike of impertinence!"

To Garten's stupefaction Ellery chose to interpret this statement as a grant of permission. He lifted one of the bags, set it on a chair, and rummaged through its contents in much the same manner as a customs inspector. Then he closed it, set the second bag on top of the first, and opened it. Across the top lay the maroon house jacket Garten had been wearing that afternoon. After a moment, Ellery's searching hands stopped. He straightened up as he took an automatic pistol from the pocket of the jacket.

After examining the pistol, Ellery said, "Mr. Garten, presumably this weapon belongs to you?"

Garten went over to him and, taking off his dark glasses, stared at the gun.

"Why, yes. Yes, it's mine, but I don't recall packing it." Puzzled, he looked from the pistol to Ellery.

"Or shooting it?" Ellery asked. "One cartridge has been fired."

"What do you mean?" Garten demanded. "I never have left it loaded in my life. Whenever I practiced with it in the basement I cleaned it and left it empty."

"Just a minute, Raymond," Griswold interrupted.

"I'll have to confess. The last time I went down to the basement I picked up your pistol by mistake. I loaded it and fired once before I noticed it was yours. I must have forgotten to unload it. I shot quite a few clips with my own."

"Does that explanation," the inspector asked ironically, "refresh your memory about packing it, Mr. Garten?"

Garten shook his head.

"Bless me if I can remember doing so."

Griswold chuckled.

"You don't know Ray Garten," he said, "or you wouldn't be surprised. He's so absent-minded that half the time he can't remember what he's been doing. When he starts puttering about he's practically in a trance—thinking about some book he's dickering for and not about what he's doing."

But Garten shook his head.

"I suppose I *must* have packed it, but— There it is. Really, it doesn't matter. I have a pistol permit."

"Unfortunately, it matters very much," Inspector Queen said quietly. "You see, Mr. Garten, John Mathews did not commit suicide. He was murdered shortly after you say you left him. If the man who we have reason to suspect is Mathews's murderer has not already been placed under arrest and confessed, I shall be obliged to ask you to come with me to headquarters for further questioning."

The inspector went to the telephone and called headquarters.

There was complete silence in the room.

After a moment, Inspector Queen said, "Hello, Captain. Any results from the alarm in the Mathews case? . . . I see. Anything new? . . . What's that? . . . *Anonymous?* When? . . . Oh, telephoned. Well, I'll be . . . No, that's just what we've done. . . . Yes, we found something. Get out a warrant at once. Yes, for *him*. Right." He put down the receiver and turned gravely to Garten.

"I'm sorry, Mr. Garten, but I am obliged to hold you. Someone telephoned in to police headquarters suggesting that a search of your apartment might throw some light on the murder of John Mathews. The tip seems to have been a good one."

Again silence. Then Griswold, his mouth open, sank into a chair.

"Look here," he said feebly, "this is an outrage. It's—it's preposterous."

Raymond Garten seemed dazed. Marian was glaring at Ellery.

"Mr. Queen," she said icily, "I suppose you think you've been as clever as you picture yourself in your books. But remember now that you're up against real people, not characters in fiction that you can push around as if they were puppets—"

"Just a minute, Marian. We must be calm," Griswold muttered. He turned upon the inspector. "Look here, Inspector, you're not dealing with gangsters or hoodlums. Mr. Garten's lawyer will be at headquarters even before you. Of course, this is all a mistake. Do you have to arrest Mr. Garten now? He won't run away!"

Inspector Queen shrugged. He looked at Garten.

"Will you come now, or would you rather wait for the warrant to be served? You can send for your lawyer, of course, if you wish."

Garten shook his head as if to clear it. Then he said with dignity: "I'll come now, Inspector Queen." He put his arm around Marian and kissed her. "Don't worry about me, my dear. When Walter calls, thank him for all he's done. Incidentally, you might tell him I didn't murder his uncle. Well, Inspector Queen?"

"Ray," Griswold said, his eyes blazing, "I'll have you

out of this tonight!" He started for the phone. "I'll call Simpson now." Halfway to the telephone he wheeled and shouted at the inspector, "You've undoubtedly heard of Gerald T. Simpson!"

"He's undoubtedly heard of *me*," Inspector Queen said. "All right, Mr. Garten. If you're ready—" To his surprise, Ellery sat down as Garten stepped towards the doorway. "Aren't you coming, El?" asked the inspector.

"No, Dad," Ellery drawled. "I think I'll stay and try to square myself with Miss Garten and—incidentally—have a chat with Mr. Griswold.

CHAPTER VIII

MYSTERY HOUSE

THE DOOR CLOSED behind Raymond Garten and Inspector Queen. Marian Garten turned furiously on Ellery.

"Mr. Queen," she choked, "you've done enough mischief for one day. I'd appreciate your leaving now, at once." She went into the hall. She came back with Ellery's hat.

Ellery lit a cigarette, smiling vaguely. He was watching Henry Griswold, who was at the telephone.

"Hello," Griswold said into the phone, "is this Mr. Simpson's residence?"

"Mr. Queen, will you *please* go!"

Seemingly unaware of the ash tray beside him, Ellery slipped the burnt match into his pocket.

"Tell him to call Henry Griswold the moment he comes in. Regent 2-6410. It's urgent." Griswold replaced the receiver and snapped to Marian, "Simpson's expected at home any minute. He'll call me," and then swinging round to face Ellery, "You're responsible for this, young man!"

Ellery said slowly, "The police suspect two people of murdering John Mathews. One is your father, Miss Garten. The other, I'm sorry to say, is Walter Mathews. There's a warrant out for him. Walter very foolishly has run away. Now, if you'll both sit down—"

But Marian had already done so. She sat staring at Ellery unbelievingly.

"Walter! They suspect *Walter?*"

Ellery told them what had happened at the Mathews house, omitting those graphic details which he felt would distress Marian. Although she kept her nerves under control, he could see plainly enough how upset she was.

"But," she asked as Ellery finished his account, "why would he run away? Of course he's innocent, but why should he *do* that?"

"To avoid being questioned," Ellery suggested.

"I don't understand, either," Griswold grumbled.

"If Walter's innocent, and I'm confident he is, what has he to hide?"

Ellery realized he must be both evasive and tactful.

"In my opinion, Walter thinks he knows—has reason to suspect—who killed his uncle. Undoubtedly he believes that whoever did is guilty of no greater crime than rendering the public a much-needed service."

"But who could have called the police and told them to search this apartment? Who could have been so foul?" Marian demanded half hysterically.

"Some crank." Ellery remained casual. "I suppose enough people know that John Mathews caused your father's ruin. They would see a motive in that."

"But," she asked quickly, "how could people know—how many people *knew* Mr. Mathews was dead?"

"That's a point," Ellery agreed. "So far as I know, only the members of the household, the murderer, of course, and the lawyer, Arthur Rhodes. Mr. Griswold, do you know this Rhodes fellow?"

"Ah!" Griswold snapped, "so *he* knew, did he? Yes, I know of him, of course. He's a crook. Don't know anything about him personally, but Walter has told us a good deal. Walter thinks his uncle put one over on Rhodes in the petroleum business."

"Rhodes has a secret yen for Carlotta Emerson," Marian interposed.

"Why secret?" Ellery asked, with sudden interest.

"Because John Mathews would never have consented to the match. She's—she was his half sister. Probably she would come into half the Mathews fortune some day. And, according to Walter, his uncle knew perfectly well that that's what Rhodes had been aiming at." Griswold jumped out of his chair as the telephone rang.

A moment later he was hurrying towards the door to the hall.

"That was Simpson. I'm going down to police headquarters with him." In the doorway he halted, hesitated, then came back, holding out his hand to Ellery. "I'm sorry, Mr. Queen, that I spoke to you as I did. It's only natural that you'd want to protect Walter. And I suppose— Oh, well, don't get any ridiculous ideas about Raymond Garten. He's incapable—utterly *incapable*—of injuring a soul." As though embarrassed by his own fervor, he quickly hurried off.

"Miss Garten," Ellery said when they were alone, "we can be fairly sure that Walter will telephone you.

If he does, I wish you would give him a message for me. Will you?"

She stared at him doubtfully. "What is it?"

"Tell him that I understand about the whistle and ask him to come to my office and tell me the whole truth. And—"

"The whistle?" Marian frowned.

"He'll know what I mean. And that when he comes I'll have to turn him over to the police. Tell him that possibly I can succeed where he'd fail and that it will be much harder for me without his help."

Marian looked bewildered.

"I'll tell him, Mr. Queen. But none of what you say makes any sense to me."

Ellery nodded. "You'll understand in time. Meanwhile, I'll do my best to persuade Dad not to hold your father. The lawyer, Simpson, will probably do more harm than good. Dad doesn't like pressure of the Blackstone variety, and nobody can tell him his business. But sometimes he listens to me." Ellery smiled. It was an infectious smile, and Marian returned it in spite of herself. "So will you do me another favor?"

"You're really going to help my father and Walter?"

she asked earnestly. "You're Walter's friend, Mr. Queen?"

"I'm doing everything I can."

"Then of course!"

"Have you a key to your old house?"

"Yes, in my purse."

"Will you let me have it?"

She looked at him searchingly for a moment. Then she went to her room and, returning, handed him a Corbin latchkey.

"What are you going to do?" she asked.

"I'm going to ask you not to go to that house again, Miss Garten, until this business has been—ah—liquidated!"

A heavy fog had rolled in from the sea. It had already enveloped Manhattan in a gray pall when Ellery Queen emerged from the apartment house where the Gartens now lived.

At Second Avenue, Ellery hailed a cab and instructed the driver to go south on the East River Drive as far as Fifty-third Street and then to return north on York Avenue.

The cab moved slowly until it reached the Drive.

Then it picked up speed. The headlights of the northbound cars penetrated the mist for scarcely more than twenty feet; they looked like the antennae of monster creeping things. The lights of the slow-moving traffic across the Queensboro Bridge cut a luminous arc in the sky. Occasionally the deep-throated reverberations of a foghorn came from some boat feeling its way through the channel in the river.

Ellery leaned out the window as the cab passed the Mathews house. Its foundations rested, twenty feet above, on top of the retaining embankment of concrete which rose sheer from the west side of the Drive. At the rear, on what he judged to be the third floor, shone a blurred patch of light—possibly from Lee's window. The dark Garten house was invisible through the mist.

The backfire of a car on the lower level of the Drive, Ellery decided as his cab sped along, would not sound too unlike a pistol shot fired in the Mathews library, if either was heard at some distance. That fact might explain why those who had heard the shot assumed that the sound came from somewhere outside the Mathews house. "It might," he repeated mentally. "But did it?"

At Fifty-seventh and Sutton Place, Ellery dismissed the cab, preferring to go the rest of the way on foot.

He approached the Garten house from the north side of the street and for a few minutes stood on the opposite sidewalk, scanning its brownstone front. A dozen steps rose to the main entrance. The steps covered the basement entrance, which was protected by an iron gate. The window shades on the parlor floor and the two stories above it were drawn. Ellery glanced westward. The dead-end street was deserted—at least as far as he could see through the fog. He crossed and went up the steps. A moment later he had quietly closed the front door behind him and, with his back to it, stood listening.

Definitely, he had heard a sound. But it was not a sound he could identify. It had been no more than a slight muffled thump coming from above. He waited several minutes without moving and then groped his way to the foot of the stairs.

He congratulated himself that, thanks to the auction, he had a fairly accurate knowledge of the parlor-floor layout. There was a sitting room to his left. Straight ahead was the door to the library where the sale had been held, and immediately to the right of it was a door to the study. The two rooms were connected by the doorway through which he had followed Nikki.

From somewhere above came an almost inaudible thump.

Ellery stood very still. Then, quite without sound, he began to climb. On the second floor enough light from the street penetrated the drawn shades so that he could see the doors left and right and the foot of the staircase which led to the third floor. Again he halted, listening.

Another sound came, after a moment or two—still from above.

But this time the sound was different. It might have been made by someone moving a chair, without lifting it, across a bare floor.

Cautiously, keeping close to the wall, Ellery resumed his climb to the third story. Despite his precautions a board creaked just as he reached the top step. He froze and again listened, leaning against what felt like a wood-paneled wall. An instant later he heard a cough. Curiously, the sound seemed to come through the wall behind him and from above.

Ellery's fingers explored the wood panel. Suddenly he realized that what he had been leaning against was not a wall but a door. But he was positive that the cough had come from above. Then the explanation dawned on him. There must be an attic that did not extend to the edge of the roof in front. That would account for its being invisible from the street. His fingers found the doorknob. He opened the door half an inch. In the dim light beyond he saw bare wooden steps. He opened the door and knelt on the bottom step. Above the top step a pale bluish streak of light showed beneath the closed door to the attic.

With infinite caution Ellery crept up the steps. He was halfway to the top, having covered the distance in complete silence, when his forehead came in contact with something that felt as light as a cobweb. Instantly something began to clatter down the steps. As it struck the landing below there was a crash of broken glass. Simultaneously the streak of light above vanished. Hurried feet thumped overhead. A moment later there was a loud bang and then absolute silence.

Ellery struck a match and climbed the remaining steps. The door at the top he found locked, but it was flimsy, constructed of thin tongue-and-groove boards held together with crosspieces. He put his shoulder against it. The door creaked and then burst open. He struck another match and looked about the room. Windowless, it was empty except for several articles lying on the dusty floor, near a ladder that extended up to a trap door in the roof.

Ellery stepped onto the first rung of the ladder and pressed against the door. Whoever had escaped through it had fastened it from the roof side. Even if it had been open, pursuit over the rooftops in the fog would have been useless. He glanced down at the collection of odds and ends at his feet—six cans of baked beans, a half-empty bottle of milk, a bag of rolls, a coffee ring on a cardboard plate, a can opener, the evening paper, a candle, and two bottles of soda water.

Ellery picked up the candle, holding it by the burnt wick, and, after wrapping it in his handkerchief, slipped it into his pocket. Then, holding a lighted match close to the floor, he examined the footprints in the dust.

Several minutes later, on his way downstairs, Ellery stopped to find out what had caused the racket that had warned the person in the attic of his approach. The device proved simple enough. With an unraveled strand of yarn stretched across one of the steps, a milk bottle had been balanced so nicely that the slightest pressure against the yarn would send the bottle clattering.

As Ellery reached the parlor floor, a loud roar reverberated through the house. What now? His first absurd thought was—a distant rumble of thunder. But the next instant he realized that it was coming from the basement.

This time he decided to throw caution to the winds. The match he was holding revealed the electric switch. He snapped on the lights. Farther down the hall, under the stairs, he found a door to the basement. He yanked it open and peered down. Through the darkness below a shaft of light swept in a broad arc, shining brilliantly against whitewashed walls, and stopped, focused on the steps. Ellery saw the electric switch at the head of the stairs. He pressed it, and the basement was flooded with light. But immediately there was a loud pop, as someone apparently struck the electric bulb, plunging the room below into darkness. Ellery could hear feet hurrying across the concrete floor below. Then came the squeak of a door being wrenched open on rusty hinges, a bang as it was slammed shut—and silence.

By the light of a match Ellery hurried down. The door to the back yard was behind the steps. He jerked it open as he blew out the match. Scarcely discernible in the mist, he could see the vague outline of a figure scaling the fence that separated the Mathews property from the Garten house. Running to the fence on tiptoe so as to make no noise, he chinned up and peered over.

No one! He pulled himself up, swinging one leg over; and then, hearing footsteps, held himself motionless. The footsteps seemed to come from the direction of the passageway that ran between the Mathews house and its neighbor. They stopped, and he surmised that whoever it was had stepped onto the soft turf in the terrace garden. The only light to be seen in the Mathews house came from the third-floor window.

Tap, tap, tap. Tap, tap, tap.

Someone was tapping at the French window.

Silence. Then the tapping began again. A light was turned on in the library. The shape of a large man sprang into view. The man's head turned, and Ellery recognized the unforgettable silhouette of Rhodes's handlebar moustache. The French window opened. The light from inside fell upon Carlotta's red hair.

"Why ah you so late?" her soft drawl demanded.

"Never mind that. They haven't caught him yet. I've been listening in on the police radio."

"Eu! Ah thought maybe y'all got lost in the fog."

"Don't be an idiot, my dear. I've got news—important news!" Rhodes went through the French window. The door closed behind him.

CHAPTER IX

An Unromantic Proposal

As Rhodes disappeared into the house, Ellery Queen slipped off the fence and returned to the Garten basement. He quickly satisfied himself concerning the cause of the rumble of distant thunder. The man—was it Rhodes?—had climbed up over the coal in the bin, and under his weight the coal had shifted. There were several tons of it. The retaining board at the end of the bin had apparently broken loose under the weight. Now half the coal was spread in an enormous pile that sloped nearly to the middle of the basement. The two irregular depressions in the coal that remained in the bin showed where the man had stood. Yes, the cause of the noise was obvious. What wasn't so obvious was why Rhodes—or anyone else, for that matter—should climb into the coal bin of the deserted Garten house.

Ellery quickly completed his examination of the basement. The shooting gallery, he found, was a passage that ran the full length of the building. Pinned to a board that was fastened to the stone foundation at the north end was a cardboard target with the bullet holes half an inch from the bull's-eye. Either Garten or Griswold was an excellent shot, Ellery decided. Judging from the position of the wooden table littered with empty cartridge boxes at the other end and the scores of empty shells on the floor about it, the distance Garten and his librarian had practiced from was forty to fifty feet. Directly above the target was a big electric bulb with a reflector.

Ellery returned to the table and examined two stacks of discarded targets. Those in one pile were initialed R.G.; in the other, H.G. It would require some study to determine whether Garten or Griswold was the better marksman. Both scores were consistently high, and in no case was a bullet hole more than four inches off the bull's-eye.

Ellery put in his pocket a target marked R.G., one marked H.G., and several empty shells, and left hurriedly by the basement door to the back yard. A few minutes later he was cautiously peering through a window of the library in the Mathews house.

Arthur Rhodes was sitting in a chair beside the fireplace with his back to the window through which Ellery was looking. At the other side of the fireplace Carlotta sat in the companion chair, facing Rhodes and Ellery. She was smiling and apparently pleased about something. Ellery could see her lips move, but he could hear nothing. He resolved to study lip-reading, a great convenience in such circumstances. Then he remembered that the first window beyond the French window had been open in the afternoon. Possibly it had been closed without being locked. He went to it and wedged the blade of his penknife between the window and the sill. Applying pressure, he slid the window up a fraction of an inch.

Slowly he raised it until he could hear voices. Carlotta and Rhodes were now out of his range of vision, but the chimpanzee, Togo, was not. The huge monk was sleeping on the floor in the same place and in much the same position that Ellery had seen Mathews's body in earlier that day. Someone had sponged the bloodstain, but the rug was still wet, and the dark blotch under Togo's head and neck recalled the scarcely less gruesome sight.

"But, Arthur, you don't have to go round and tap any moah," Ellery heard Carlotta say. "Why didn't you ring the bell tonight?"

"I thought Queen might have posted a man in the hall to keep an eye on things. It's just as well to be discreet for a while, you know."

"There's no reason, reahly. They searched the place with a fine-tooth comb and then cleahed out, thank Heaven!"

Ellery heard a match scratch, and for a moment there was silence. Blue smoke drifted towards the window. It curled out through the crack, and he smelled the heavy aroma of cigar smoke.

Then Rhodes's guttural voice asked: "Why didn't you tell the police you saw Garten across the way about the time John was shot?"

"You know why, silly."

"Because of Walter?"

"Naturally. If he's convicted—"

"He'd be electrocuted, and you'd be the sole heir instead of the recipient of a $5,000 annuity."

"Don't be so crude, Arthur. You know Ah'm fond of Walter—"

"Skip it, Carlotta. It doesn't matter now."

"What doesn't?"

"Whom they pin the murder on—or whether they decide it was suicide. So if you're wise you'll tell them about Garten. Give them something to think about."

"But how do you mean, it doesn't matter? As next of kin, I'd be John's legal heir, if it weren't for Walter. You told me that yourself. It was your idea to get him out of the way."

Remarkable how the Southern accent had vanished!

"Not exactly mine." There was pronounced sarcasm in his tone. "But anyhow, the scheme worked even better than we hoped, and you can rejoice in the prospect of becoming my wife."

Carlotta laughed. It was the shrill laugh of an adolescent girl.

"Don't flattah yourself, Mistah Rhodes. We were working togethah on a strictly business basis. Besides, your cigah is suffocating me." And there it was—back again.

"Well, smoke yourself and you won't notice it."

"Eu! I left my cigarettes upstairs. Togo! Togo!" she called.

The chimpanzee rolled half over and looked at her. His eyes looked like two beads set in the middle of gray saucers.

"Togo!"

Togo scratched himself behind the ear and sat up.

"Cigarettes, Togo. Go on. Get Carlo her cig-ah-rettes."

Apparently she was gesticulating, for Rhodes said, "You should have been a pantomimist, my dear."

"Good Togo. Go on. Cigarettes, Togo."

The chimpanzee got up and on all fours lumbered off through the doorway to the drawing room.

"Keep it on a business basis if you wish, Carlo," Rhodes went on. "It's all the same to me. But the fact remains that you're going to marry me, and immediately after the ceremony you're going to transfer half of John's estate to me."

Carlotta gasped.

"Say," she said—gone again!—"what are you talking about, Arthur?"

"Perhaps I haven't all the charm that you'd desire in a husband," he chuckled, "but I have brains. You'll have to admit that."

"Not judging from the way you let John put it over on you in the oil deal," she retorted.

"What did that matter, since we get the whole works anyhow?"

Togo reappeared in the doorway, his long black fingers wrapped about a package of cigarettes. Moving awkwardly on his hind legs, he moved away, disappearing from Ellery's sight.

Rhodes laughed.

"Nice Togo. Good Togo," Carlotta cooed. A match scratched. "Careful, now. *That's* righty. Noney *bur*ny! Nice Togo. There! Carlo's nice Togo."

To Ellery's astonishment the chimp came lumbering back with a lighted cigarette in his hand. He leaped up into the chair before which he had been lying and, leaning against the desk, puffed—or rather, sucked—the cigarette. He thrust it for half its length between his thick lips and, after sucking it, held it at arm's length while he blew the smoke out.

"You'd better tell me what you're talking about," Carlotta was saying.

"It's all very simple, my dear. I have John's wills—the one he made some time ago, about which I told you—"

"Leaving everything to Walter except the $5,000 a year to me?" she asked angrily.

"Exactly. And another he signed this afternoon."

"What? You didn't tell me. Why didn't you tell me?" she asked breathlessly. "What did he do? What changes did he make?"

"Very radical changes, my dear. He cut Walter out of it entirely."

"Then I'm—"

"You're the sole heir—or can be if you wish."

"But I am or I'm not," she said impatiently. "Why do you have to be so exasperating?"

"It merely depends on whether you marry me and sign certain papers, that's all."

"But if he made the will—"

"Which will is probated depends entirely on me, Carlo."

"But there must have been witnesses. You can't—"

"Can't I, my dear?" he interrupted. "All I have to do is to say that when John phoned me this afternoon he instructed me to destroy the last will. It's as simple as that."

Carlotta was speechless.

After a moment, Rhodes said gruffly, "If the idea of being my wife is so distasteful to you, forget it. The fact that Walter is under suspicion is all to the good. I can get him out of that mess and make a multimillionaire out of him. Yes, perhaps I can make a better deal with him than I can with you!"

Behind Ellery the mist suddenly became bright. He turned quickly and saw that the lights had been turned on in the Garten library. A moment later he had swung himself over the fence and was hurrying towards the basement door.

CHAPTER X

SHYSTER

THE FIRST THING Ellery Queen recalled when he awoke in the morning was the expression on Velie's face when the sergeant suddenly saw him emerge from the basement of the Garten house. Velie and two plainclothes men had arrived a few minutes past eleven to search the place, and the last thing the sergeant expected to find was Ellery. His mouth had opened to form almost as large a circle, Ellery thought, as the face of Big Ben.

Ellery saw that it was only seven-thirty. He lit a cigarette and lay back lazily to think. At the Garten house the night before, he had asked Velie to have the coal in the basement thoroughly sifted in an effort to learn why the second intruder had climbed up on it. Later

Velie had reported to Inspector Queen at headquarters, where Ellery had gone to talk with his father, that a small leather case with Mr. Garten's name had been found under the coal. The case contained a telescopic sight. The sergeant had seen many a telescopic sight in his day, he declared, but never any quite like this. It was not designed for a rifle, apparently, but possibly for a pistol.

Garten had readily admitted owning the sight, but insisted that he had not seen it in weeks and had used it only once. He had picked it up when he was traveling in Europe, years before, and brought it home as a curiosity. One day he tried it out and found that it could be used with remarkable accuracy if he rested the barrel of the pistol on something firm. Otherwise it was almost impossible to press the trigger quickly enough when the sight was on the target. Besides, he could see no use for it. A target for pistol range was close enough, anyhow. It wasn't sporting to use the gadget. The last time he'd seen it was when Rhodes, Mathews's lawyer, had come to call about the petroleum investments. Garten had been down in the shooting range with Griswold, and Rhodes had joined him there. Rhodes had picked up the sight and asked what it was.

SHYSTER

The case against Garten, Ellery decided, was tightening, although he had established an alibi of a sort. Garten said that at ten minutes past six of the fateful afternoon he was in a cigar store at Madison Avenue near Fifty-ninth Street. The clerk knew him because he had frequently bought cigarettes there. The clerk confirmed the statement. But while the alibi would hold if the shot that killed Mathews was fired a few seconds before Walter called the police, as Walter swore it was, it did not hold if, as the others testified, the shot had been fired just before six o'clock. Moreover, according to what Carlotta Emerson told Rhodes, Garten was in his house some time later than he admitted having been there.

At the recollection of Rhodes's conversation with Carlotta, Ellery got out of bed. He would work for an hour or so at his office and then call on Rhodes.

And Walter, Ellery wondered as he pulled off his pajama top—wouldn't Walter be acting the same way if he were guilty? Obviously he was trying to draw a red herring across the trail to the murderer. But suppose he—Walter—was guilty himself? Then might he not with even greater cunning try to appear to do just that so as to divert suspicion to someone else? Walter was smart. The fingerprints on the candle Ellery had taken from the Garten attic proved that it was Walter who had fled through the trap door. He'd certainly been smart about choosing his hiding place. The last place in the world the police would think of looking for him would be within a hundred feet of the place he'd escaped from. They would comb the whole country for him before they would think of looking in the Garten attic. And if they did become suspicious of Garten and search the house, Walter had his escape all prepared. Moreover, he would know if the police came there that Garten must be suspected. Was that his game? Well, it was all to the good, if so, that the inspector had released Garten after questioning him. It would just about checkmate Walter, and he'd have to come out from cover.

But no, Walter couldn't have tried to frame Raymond Garten. The impression on the rug in the Mathews library proved that. Ellery opened a bureau drawer and selected a white shirt.

He remembered the novel he was working on. He'd promised it to his publisher on the fifteenth. If Nikki actually had the crust to come in late this morning ...

Nikki Porter, to Ellery's surprise, was blithely tapping at the keys of her typewriter when he opened the door to his office.

The keys stopped clicking, however, the moment he entered.

"Oh, Ellery," she said, getting quickly up from her chair, "I'm so thrilled! I've started a new book—a mystery. My very own! I'm calling it *Murder in the Library*. Isn't that a grand title?"

"Have you finished those chapters I left for you?" he demanded as he strode by her desk on the way to his office.

"Of course, Ellery—last night. I worked awfully late, even after your Miss Garten called. Is she really engaged to Walter Mathews? What's she like, Ellery? She sounded awfully nice. Blonde, I suppose?"

Ellery sighed as he sat down at his desk.

"Yes, blonde. So what?"

"Oh, nothing," Nikki said, coming into the private office. "How do you like my permanent?"

"It's all right," he said, without looking up.

"Ellery."

"Yes—"

"You've got to help me."

"What now?"

"This Mathews case. You've got to tell me all about it. I'm going to use it for my mystery."

Ellery groaned.

"Nikki, for Pete's sake, forget about writing *your* mystery stories and remember mine! You know you never—"

"Ellery." She trailed fingers across the hair waving back from his forehead. "You look so handsome when— You see, I've really got it started. You mustn't be conceited. You aren't the only person who can write mystery stories. You will tell me, won't you?"

From experience Ellery had learned that with Nikki more time was wasted by resistance than by acquiescence. It was nearly ten o'clock when he finished telling her about the Mathews case—the perfect or almost perfect crime, he added, looking thoughtfully out the window.

Nikki took shorthand notes while he talked, half to himself, half to her, all the while trying to fit the details into the pattern of his theory that he felt must inevitably lead to the solution of the crime.

At a few minutes past ten, after Nikki had gone back to her typewriter, Ellery rose with the announcement that he was going out.

"Where to, Ellery?" she asked.

"To have a chat with Arthur Rhodes. His office is on Fifty-seventh Street," he told her. "I'll call you as soon as I leave him. It's just possible that Walter might come in or telephone. If he shows up, hold him, no matter what you have to do."

"Don't worry," Nikki answered him, her eyes shining. "Just let him try to get away!"

As Ellery took his hat from the clothes tree in the corner of the office and started towards the door, Nikki suddenly said, "Ellery, you poor lamb, you've missed the whole point. I *know* how Mr. Mathews was killed. It's as plain as ABC. Oh, you simple-minded men! You'll never know anything about women!"

But Ellery did not hear her. He was absorbed in thoughts of how best to approach Arthur Rhodes.

In the building at the corner of Fifty-seventh Street and Lexington Avenue, Rhodes's office was on the twenty-third floor. A blonde receptionist at the switchboard, trying to conceal the fact that she was chewing gum, announced Ellery over the phone. Then she turned to him.

"Mr. Rhodes will see you in a moment, Mr. Queen. Won't you please sit down?"

She motioned towards an uninviting bench beside a

bare table in the reception hall and returned avidly to her magazine.

The telephone rang. "Yes, Mr. Rhodes." The blonde said to Ellery, "Mr. Rhodes will see you now, Mr. Que-en," and smiled.

Arthur Rhodes was seated behind a large flat-top desk facing the door through which Ellery entered. Behind him, law books in their monotonously uniform bindings lined the wall to the ceiling. A long, unlighted cigar, from which he had not removed the red and gold band, protruded aggressively from the corner of Rhodes's mouth.

"Oh, it's you, is it?" he said irritably. "The girl said Mr. Queen. I thought she meant your father."

"Were you expecting him?" Uninvited, Ellery sat down in a chair at the opposite side of the desk from Rhodes and deftly sailed his fedora hat onto a hook of the clothes tree where hung Rhodes's black derby.

Rhodes's black hair was pasted down almost as evenly as was the hard felt of the derby hat, Ellery noticed, and the tips of his handlebar moustache were waxed.

"Well, yes and no." Rhodes bit off the end of the cigar and spat it into the scrapbasket. He rolled the cigar band into a wad and tossed it out the window. "Being John Mathews's attorney, I thought he might call. What can I do for you, Queen?"

"I believe you said yesterday that Mr. Mathews phoned you at five-forty in the afternoon."

"That's right."

"And that you had previously left him at three-ten, having obtained his signature to a new will?"

"Right."

"Did he imply in any way that something might have occurred between three-ten and the time he called you to make him change his mind about the new will?"

"No."

"He didn't mention, for instance, that he had been talking with Walter just a few minutes before?"

"No. . . . In just what way does all this concern you, Mr. Queen?" Rhodes's eyes narrowed as he looked across the desk at Ellery.

"I'm asking these questions on behalf of my client."

"Your client? Who's your client?"

"Walter Mathews."

Rhodes struck a match, lighted the cigar, and puffed thoroughly at it.

"I had no idea you were a lawyer, Mr. Queen. I was under the impression that you're a writer—of mystery stories," he added contemptuously.

"Once in a while I try my hand at criminal investigation," Ellery murmured. "In the blood, you know. Good fun. Besides, there's pleasure in the extermination of vermin."

"I see. I take it you, too, think John Mathews was murdered. Well, there are plenty of people John wasn't popular with—besides his nephew."

"Yes, I understand Mathews let you down pretty hard in your last deal together."

Although Rhodes shrugged indifferently, Ellery could see that he had prodded a sore spot.

"He sold out before I did, if that's what you mean."

"In the new will, is Miss Emerson the chief legatee?" Ellery asked suddenly.

Rhodes pretended to be shocked.

"My dear Mr. Queen, you must realize that as the late John Mathews's attorney— Why! Such things are sacred confidences in my profession."

"Sorry to have offended your sensibilities," Ellery said, smiling. "Was it your sensibilities, too, that kept you from telling Inspector Queen about your having gone back into the house immediately after you left Mr. Mathews?"

Rhodes held his breath a moment.

"What do you mean?" he blustered.

"That you were admitted by Miss Emerson. How long did you remain?"

"Now, look here, Queen!" Rhodes began. But then he said, "I don't see any reason why I shouldn't be frank with you, though I must admit I resent your intrusion into my affairs. Miss Emerson and I are engaged. We went down to the Municipal Building and applied for the marriage license this morning. Yes, after leaving John, I did return for a word with Carlotta. I remained possibly five minutes. But I repeat, that's none of your business. And it has no bearing on the case at hand. None whatsoever!"

"Well, it might," Ellery mused. "For instance, if you told her the good news that she was Mr. Mathews's sole heir or principal heir and that Walter was entirely cut out of the will, then it's only repetitious to say that she and not Walter would benefit by Mathews's death."

"But I didn't tell her that was what John had done!" Too late, Rhodes saw his blunder. "I'm sorry, Queen," he said, thumping the desk, "but I'll have to ask you to leave. I'm busy." Abruptly he got up from his chair.

"I think," Ellery said quietly, "that first you had better show me the will, my dear sir. Either you will satisfy me that the signature is genuine, so that I can assure my client of the fact, or I shall have to report the possibility of a conspiracy between you and Miss Emerson to the district attorney."

Rhodes glared at Ellery.

Ellery continued, "Mr. Mathews's death, his making of a new will, and your sudden engagement to the heir, all seem astonishingly well timed. Forgive me; 'coincidental' might be a kinder word."

"Are you suggesting that the signature is a forgery?" Rhodes demanded indignantly.

"If you let me see it and I find it to be genuine, then I shall assume that the will is of no interest to the district attorney, and I shall not have to ask him to investigate on Walter's behalf."

Rhodes did not see the trap. The best thing to do was to humor this persistent nuisance and get him out of the office. He went to his safe, opened the steel door, and dug out an envelope.

"Here, here's the signature." He came to Ellery, held the will up. "Are you satisfied?"

Ellery glanced at John Mathews's signature, which he had never seen before in his life and so was quite incapable of judging its authenticity; and he glanced, too, at the signatures of the witnesses.

"Thanks," he said, getting up. "It was the will itself, not the signature, that I wanted to see, so that I could swear to its existence. You, as a lawyer, will realize the seriousness of the offense now if the will is destroyed. You will hereafter willingly co-operate with me until the murder of John Mathews is cleared up. Otherwise I shall inform Miss Emerson that you are powerless to destroy the will. And I don't imagine that you will win either your bride or half her inheritance unless you can threaten her with its destruction."

Rhodes was stunned. He stared stupidly as Ellery took his hat from the clothes tree and, with a polite nod, strolled from the office.

CHAPTER XI

Cherchez la Femme

When Ellery reached the street he went immediately to a telephone booth and called his office.

"Nikki, has Walter called?"

"No, Ellery, but—"

"Marian Garten?"

"Yes, Ellery, but—"

"What did she say?"

"That the police have been questioning the Negro telephone operator at her apartment house about Walter's phone call and that she's terribly upset. But, Ellery—"

"Get it off your chest."

"I know who killed Mr. Mathews."

"What?"

"I *do*. I'm sure of it!"

"Get back to work and stop dreaming."

"But I do! How can I work when I know who the murderer is? I started my new book—the one about the Mathews murder, you know. Did the outline. Then all of a sudden it came to me. In a flash, Ellery! What's more, I can *prove* it."

"Prove what?"

"Who murdered him, silly!"

Ellery sighed.

"All right. Who murdered whom?"

"Ellery."

"Yes."

"I'm serious."

"Yes, Nikki."

"Dead serious."

"Yes."

"Ellery, can you meet me in front of the Mathews house right away?"

"Why?"

"You've got to, Ellery."

"But why?"

"I'll tell you when I see you. I can't over the phone. Hurry, Ellery. I'll be there in ten minutes. Please."

"Nikki—"

Ellery heard a click. Blast!

Nikki was leaning against the low wall above the East River Drive when Ellery got out of the cab before the Mathews house. She looked very fetching in something cloudy blue. Not the least like a lady detective. Not the least like anything but a cute nuisance!

"Well, you got here at last," she said as he strode up to her.

"Now, look here, Nikki. A joke's a joke—"

"Ellery, you've overlooked the first principle of detection."

"Which is?"

"Cherchez la femme."

Ellery groaned.

"She did it, Ellery. I'm positive."

"Who?" he asked, scowling down at the traffic on the Drive.

"Carlotta Emerson, of course. At least, she's *responsible*."

"You mean she planned it with Rhodes?"

"Maybe he's in it, too. I don't know. Yes, maybe he is. But anyhow, she's the murderer, really. Don't you see, she's the one with the strongest motive? The new will left everything to her."

"But she didn't know about the new will—not until

Rhodes told her last night," Ellery pointed out dryly.

She looked at him pityingly.

"You poor dodo! Of course she'd pretend not to know—especially since she murdered him."

"But how could she know?" he demanded.

Nikki sighed.

"Naturally she'd worm it out of John Mathews. Don't you know *anything* about women? And isn't it natural that he would tell her? He was mad at Walter, wasn't he? Well, if he was, he'd tell her; he'd *want* her to know. She's the kind that coos at men, isn't she? 'Eu,' she says, 'reahly.' I know *her* kind. The daddums type. The big—mare! Anyway, even if he didn't tell her, she had her ear to the keyhole all the time Rhodes was talking with Mr. Mathews."

"All right, Nikki. Let's argue that Carlotta might have known. The next step, please!" Ellery was annoyed that the possibility of Carlotta's knowing about the will had not occurred to him. Perhaps she had been putting on an act for Rhodes's benefit and had taken him in, too.

"The next step?" Nikki threw back her head and trilled silvery laughter. "Do you mean to say you don't see it *yet*?"

"I take it you think that while Walter was upstairs, getting his wrist watch and gloves, Carlotta came down and shot Mathews."

Nikki was thoughtful for a moment.

"I hadn't thought of that," she admitted.

"If she did she would have met Walter. She couldn't have got back to her room."

"Oh! Of course. That's right, Ellery. I did think of it; I remember now. That's what put me onto the track of how she did it."

"And just how was that?" he asked patiently.

"The chimp!"

"The chimp?"

"Yes! Togo. The monkey you told me about. She trained him to get her cigarettes—and everything else. Why couldn't she train him to shoot a gun?"

Ellery laughed.

"Nikki, for the love of William Tell! Don't be absurd."

"But it's *not* absurd. Carlotta sent the chimp down the rainpipe, or whatever you call it, to shoot Mathews. She sent Togo the moment she heard Walter come up to his room. She'd been listening to the row and knew that when Walter heard the shot he'd go running back to the library. Then Togo would be back up in her room by the time he got there. Naturally, Walter would think his uncle had killed himself."

"Whoa. Let's go back to the beginning. How could she possibly have trained Togo to shoot a pistol without everyone in the neighborhood knowing about it?"

"Oh, Ellery, at times you're positively obtuse. Of course, she wouldn't train him with a *loaded* gun. She'd teach him to aim it and pull the trigger while it was empty. Haven't you ever seen boys with toy pistols? They squint along the barrel with the gun pointed at you, and then it goes click. Weren't you ever a little boy, Ellery?"

He laughed again. The idea was preposterous—but in a way it wasn't. Ellery remembered how important a part a raven had played in the mysterious death of one John Braun. If a raven—

"And I suppose," he asked ironically, "she taught Togo to put the gun down by the dead man's left hand because he was left-handed?"

"Of course not. I'll explain that in a minute. Tell me, were there fingerprints on the pistol?"

"John Mathews's and some blurred prints that couldn't be identified. Walter's weren't on it, but that doesn't mean anything. He could have worn the gloves."

"Then Carlotta must have taken Mr. Mathews's gun and given it to the chimp. Yes, that explains everything. Did the police fingerprint the monkey?"

Ellery had a mental picture of Velie taking the chimpanzee's fingerprints.

"I'm afraid they overlooked him," he said gravely. "Is your case complete, Miss Porter?"

"Well, I'll explain how the pistol came to be left behind on the floor after Togo shot Mathews," Nikki said thoughtfully. "She'd trained him, you see, with an unloaded pistol. This time it was loaded. It went off with a bang that scared the chimp out of seven years' growth. Naturally he'd drop it like a hot poker and tear back to his mistress as fast as he could."

Ellery said briskly, "Theory's ingenious, Nikki. But it simply doesn't jibe with Walter's actions after Mathews was murdered. For example—"

"Do I have to explain everything?" said Nikki crossly. "Can't you do *any* thinking for yourself? Whether his behavior conforms to your notions of what Walter would do doesn't matter. What matters is whether the fingerprints check."

"What fingerprints?"

"The chimp's, of course. Are you going to come with me, or do I have to go alone?"

"Go where?"

"I'm going to get a sample of Togo's prints so that your father can check them with the smudged ones on the pistol."

"Just how are you going to do that?"

She opened her purse and showed him a silver cigarette case.

"I'm going to offer him a cigarette and hand him this. His prints will be on the case. I've planned the whole thing, Ellery. It makes no difference to me whether you're afraid to come or not. I'm going to pretend to be a reporter, and while I'm interviewing Miss Emerson, I'll ask about her pet. I'll ask her to show it to me. There were pictures of Togo in the morning papers. I'm going to be a society reporter."

"You'll never get in, Nikki. Any interviews there were were over the phone."

"Oh, I'll get in," she said, "if nobody's locked that window in the library!" She hurried off towards the Mathews house—very fetching in cloudy blue, and looking less like a lady detective, if that were possible, than ever.

Ellery was thoughtful. Nikki's "theories" had got her into trouble before. He stood, scowling, until she disappeared in the passageway between the buildings, and then started reluctantly after her.

Apparently she had run the moment she was out of sight, for she was not in the passage when he reached it. At a dog trot he went towards the terrace garden in the rear.

Nikki had the window up and one leg over the sill when he reached her.

"So you decided to come?" she asked scornfully in a whisper and slid into the Mathews library.

Ellery climbed in after her.

"I don't see that I've had any choice," he mumbled. "You're not a secretary—you're a problem child!" But Nikki paid no attention.

"Now you wait for me here, Ellery. I'll go up alone. She won't talk if you're there. Her room is the first at the right, at the top of the stairs, isn't it?"

"No, that's Walter's. Carlotta's is opposite. Have you a notebook?"

She tapped her purse.

"Yes, stenographic. And I wrote myself some credentials from the *Evening Dispatch*. Don't worry, I've planned everything. If she comes down with me, pretend you don't know me. Then I'll meet you at the office." She tiptoed through the doorway to the drawing room.

Ellery closed the window through which they had climbed. He glanced down at the faded stain on the rug before the chair. After a moment he crossed to the refectory table behind the couch that faced the fireplace.

The volume entitled *Wills and Testaments* near the right end of the row of books on the table had been pushed back in line with the others. He leaned over and pulled it out about three inches; he looked to the right; he looked to the left. Apparently satisfied, he went to the French window, peered out.

The basement door of the Garten house was hidden behind the fence. The east windows of the house were almost in a direct line with a path that led from the middle of the French window in the Mathews house. Because of the bend in the East River and consequently in the Drive, the east end of the Garten house stood about ten feet west of the Mathews place. The Garten house had three windows on each floor. The windows of the Garten library, where the auction sale had been held, were on a level with the top of the fence.

Ellery stepped back several feet, knelt. From the second-floor windows of the Garten house one could see, he decided, no further into this room than the edge of the rug. From the top floor you wouldn't be able to see into the room at all. He got to his feet and began to pace restlessly back and forth. He became conscious of the dull ticking of the clock on the mantel above the fireplace and the monotonous hum of traffic on the Drive....

Eleven-forty-seven.

Nikki had been gone five minutes. Apparently she was having her "interview" successfully. But—

Ellery's restlessness increased. It wasn't just restlessness; it was nervousness. He stopped pacing and listened—just the hum and the ticking....

Eleven-fifty.

But what if Nikki were right? Not about Carlotta's having trained Togo to commit the murder—though that possibility couldn't be eliminated entirely if another motive lay behind Walter's actions. But suppose Carlotta herself—Rhodes— Oh, blast it! Why had he let her go upstairs at all? What if Carlotta saw through her masquerade? What if she saw that Nikki was on the right track? Her gun had disappeared. Or had it?

She might have hidden it and pretended that someone had taken it.

Ellery glanced at the clock again.

Eleven-fifty-four.

He went into the drawing room and stood by the settee, listening. An automobile horn honked somewhere in the street. A boy outside was calling, "Jim-may! Oh, Jim-may! Bring the football!"

He walked into the hall, made for the stairs. With one foot on the bottom step and his hand on the newel post, he listened intently.

"Jim-may! Aw, say, Jim, come on."

The door to Carlotta's room must be closed. No sound came down the stairs.

He'd wait two more minutes, and then he'd go up and end this idiotic suspense.

He waited less than a minute.

The scream that seared his nerves came, beyond any doubt, from Nikki's white throat.

"Don't! Don't! Stop!" Her voice was harsh with terror.

As Ellery sprang forward, a pistol went off. It was followed by a series of cries so terrified they seemed unhuman. They stopped abruptly as Ellery reached the floor above. He leaped across the hall and crashed through the door to Carlotta Emerson's room.

Her face bloodless, her stiff fingers clutching the lavender spread she had half dragged from the bed, Nikki lay on the floor.

Staring down at her with dilated eyes—Carlotta, a pistol in her hand. She swayed at the crash of Ellery's entrance. Her fingers relaxed, and the pistol slipped from them. With a little thump it landed on the rug.

CHAPTER XII

Confession

NIKKI'S EYES fluttered open. The look of terror that sprang into them changed to one of bewilderment as she stared up at Ellery. He was kneeling beside her.

"It murdered— I was— Ellery—" She sat up abruptly, clutched his arm. Wild-eyed once more, she pointed to something behind him. "Ellery, look!"

Turning, Ellery saw the chimpanzee. His broad back turned towards them, Togo was cowering in the corner, arms wrapped over his head.

Carlotta Emerson sank onto the edge of her bed.

"Nikki, what happened?" Ellery demanded. "Are you hurt?"

"I don't know," she moaned. "I thought I was dead—

that I'd been shot. That creature tried to *murder* me."

"Thank Heaven, he missed her." Carlotta put her trembling finger to her lips. "I grabbed for the gun just as it went off."

In the corner Togo began to whimper. Ellery felt for the pistol; it was safely in his pocket.

"What happened?" he asked, helping Nikki to her feet.

"The beast tried to kill me," she said, calmer now. "Look there." She pointed the tip of her shoe at a hole, about the size of a dime, in the rug. The edges of the hole were singed, and the area about it for several inches was speckled with powder burns. "It missed me, all right. That's the bullet hole."

"Yes." Carlotta's voice was shaky. "I caught the gun by the barrel and pointed it down."

"Where did the gun come from?" Ellery asked. "How did the monkey get it?"

"I don't know."

"He came through the window with it," Nikki said. "He waved it all around, and then he saw me and came towards me, pointing it at me. And—oh!" She gasped and turned white.

Togo with a single bound had sprung halfway across

the room. With a second leap, he landed on the window sill. An instant later he appeared to swing out into space and vanished.

Ellery ran to the window and looked out. With amazing speed the chimpanzee was clambering up the drainpipe. In a moment it had reached the gutter and swung itself onto the roof.

"Miss Emerson," Ellery asked, closing the window, "how did your chimpanzee learn to shoot?"

"I don't know," she said, still trembling, "unless—"

"Unless what?"

"Sometimes he used to sit on the back fence, watching Mr. Garten and Mr. Griswold practice in their basement."

Ellery turned to Nikki.

"Are you sure Togo had the pistol when he came through the window?"

"Of course!"

"He must have taken it from the drawer," Carlotta said. "Sometimes he hides things on the roof."

"I'll be back in a minute," Ellery said, starting for the door. "I'm going to take a look around up there."

When Ellery stepped out onto the roof, Togo was squatting by the chimney, munching an apple core. He stopped to glare suspiciously when he saw Ellery. But he made no hostile move.

The monkey had collected its treasures, Ellery soon discovered, in the gutter overhanging the front of the house. Here he had cached a pair of rubbers, a hot-water bottle, a small watering pot—the one Velie had mentioned, Ellery guessed—a piece of chalk, and a whiskbroom. It was quite possible, he decided, that the pistol had been part of the collection.

He was examining the articles that Togo had filched when two police cars drew up to the curb before the house.

The door of the first car opened and Sergeant Velie heaved out. He held the door open as Inspector Queen stepped to the sidewalk. The inspector was followed by a plainclothes man and Raymond Garten. Then, with a start, Ellery noticed the two men who had got out of the second car. They were Detective Flint and, handcuffed to his wrist, Walter Mathews, hatless and bedraggled.

Ellery hurried back to Carlotta's room. Despite Nikki's angry protests that she would not leave before getting a sample of Togo's prints, he sent her back to the office. Then he went to the library, where he found his father, Velie, Flint, and their two prisoners.

The inspector immediately took Ellery aside.

"Now listen, son," he said grumpily. "I'm conducting a little experiment here, and I don't want any interference, understand? This case is about to break! Not a word out of you, no matter what anyone does or says."

"Did I say no?" Ellery said amiably.

Inspector Queen focused his bright little eyes on Walter, who, unshaven and bleary-eyed, looked as if he had not slept for days.

"Now, Mathews, I'm going to ask you to repeat your answers to a few questions I've already asked you. I want you to think carefully and, if you're not positive about any point, to say so frankly."

Walter nodded wearily, glanced at Ellery, shrugged. He was dejected and dull-eyed.

"When you arrived here yesterday to see your uncle, what time was it?"

"Five-forty-three."

"You quarreled with your uncle and threatened to expose him, did you not?"

"I've told you that right along."

"Leaving Mr. Mathews, you went up to your room to get your gloves?"

"My watch," Walter said. "I happened to see my gloves, so I took them, too."

"Where were they?"

"In my bureau drawer."

"Do you own a gun?" the inspector asked sharply.

"Yes."

"Where do you keep it?"

"In my bureau drawer."

"The same drawer that you saw your watch and gloves in?"

"Yes."

"Was the gun in the drawer then?"

"Yes."

"Did you take it out?"

"No, not then."

"When did you?"

"Afterwards—when Flint took me up to my room. I asked him to call Lee and order some coffee and a sandwich. Flint went into the hallway for a moment, and I took the pistol then."

Detective Flint cleared his throat, but the inspector glared at him.

"Why?"

"Because your men had taken my wallet and everything I had in my pockets when they searched me. I'd decided to get away, and I didn't have a red cent for food. I knew I could pawn the gun."

"How long were you upstairs after leaving your uncle—when you got your watch, that is?"

"Half a minute, maybe."

"When you came down you saw him taking a gun out of that table drawer?" The inspector pointed to the table by the window. "You ran for the street and had just reached the door when you heard the shot?"

"Yes."

"Then you immediately telephoned police headquarters?"

"Yes."

"All right, Mathews. Flint, take him up to his room and wait until I send for you." The inspector took the handcuff that dangled from Walter's wrist and clamped it around the detective's. "If you go out the window this time, you'll have to take Flint with you."

Flint jerked Walter towards the door.

"Come on," they heard the detective mutter. "And no tricks. I'm sick of being the patsy!"

Half dragged, Walter stumbled out of the room.

During the questioning, Ellery had not been watching Walter, but Garten, whose confidence of the previous day had quite vanished. In less than twenty hours, he appeared to have aged several years. The pouches below his dark glasses were grayer, and his cheeks hung flabbily. Occasionally he had started at Walter's answers and had almost continuously run his fingers through his sparse gray hair. His distress had become especially evident during Walter's testimony about the pistol. Now, lost in thought, it was a moment or two before he realized that Inspector Queen was speaking to him.

"Do you see, Mr. Garten," the inspector asked a second time, "how the evidence is piling up against Walter Mathews?"

"Yes . . . yes . . .," Garten said absently.

The inspector turned to Velie.

"All right, Sergeant, show Mr. Garten the bullet."

"Yes, sir." Sergeant Velie held up a flattened lump of lead. "You see, Mr. Garten, we figure it this way. We found the bullet in your yard near the east end of the house. It must of squashed itself out against the back of the house. Dead man was layin' there where you see the spot on the rug. He was sittin' in the desk chair, and he was shot from some place near the kidney table." The sergeant's long finger pointed in successive directions to indicate the objects he mentioned. "At first we thought the bullet might of gone in the river, because it went out the window in that direction. But the doc said after the p.m. that it could of been deflected when it hit Mathews's neck."

"O.K., Velie," Inspector Queen said. "Mr. Garten, the shot that killed Mathews was fired a little before six. Walter is lying when he says it was fired later. There are two possible explanations for the lie. The first is that he was waiting for a chance to get away. The butler was outside on the sidewalk. He may have waited for him to go back inside. But the butler stayed there until the Chinese servant came down at seven minutes past six, to find Walter at the phone."

"I see," Garten said tonelessly. "And the other explanation?"

"Just a minute." Inspector Queen opened the door to the drawing room. "Come in, please, Miss Emerson."

Carlotta, her self-possession completely restored, came into the room. She saw Raymond Garten, stopped short, looked quickly away from him.

"Miss Emerson," the inspector said, "when I talked with you this morning you gave me further details about what you did and what you saw late yesterday afternoon. Having refreshed your memory, you recalled that at the time you heard the shot you had already finished your nap and had gotten up. Is that correct?"

"Yes, Inspectuh Queen."

"What did you see?"

"I saw Mr. Garten pacin' up and down in his lib'ary."

"Thank you, Miss Emerson. That's all."

"Eu," she said and swept by the sergeant, who had opened the door for her with Gargantuan gallantry.

Inspector Queen crossed the room and stood facing Garten.

"The man at the cigar store says the only reason he has for believing that you were in his shop at the time you said you were, Garten, is because you *yourself* took out your watch, looked at it, and mentioned the time. It's conceivable that you added or subtracted five or ten minutes in order to give yourself an alibi. That brings us to the second possible reason for Walter's delay in telephoning the police."

Garten started violently and then sank back into the chair.

"That's enough, Inspector," he muttered. "I didn't believe it possible for you to trump up such a watertight case against the boy. Don't think that I regret killing Mathews. He deserved what he got, and I'm glad I've rid the world of him. I thought maybe I could get away with it without paying the penalty. But since I must, I must. Yes, I killed him. I came back over the fence. I'd gone home to get my pistol. Then I began to think. I remembered that Mathews kept one here. That must have been when Miss Emerson saw me pacing in the library. I decided to use his pistol and make it look like suicide. Walter came in while I was placing the pistol on the floor. He could see at a glance what it was all about. He must have waited before phoning you so that I could get away and establish an alibi." He rose, pale but resolute. "Now, Inspector Queen, I'll willingly sign a confession, but only on one condition, and if you don't grant that condition I'll repudiate what I've just told you and fight the case. You'll save the State a lot of money if you'll agree."

"What's the condition?"

"That you release Walter Mathews and give me your word of honor no charges will be brought against him."

The inspector appeared to consider the proposal.

After a moment he said, "If Walter agrees to testify against you, I have no doubt the district attorney will be willing to play ball."

"Sorry," Garten said curtly. "I'm afraid that won't do. I want your word for it, Queen."

"Pardon me," Ellery said before his father could answer. He paused to light a cigarette, and they had to wait for him. "Mr. Garten, will you accept *my* word for it instead of my father's?"

"Thank you, Mr. Queen," Garten said firmly, "but you're hardly in a position to pledge the integrity of the prosecuting attorney."

Ellery turned to his father.

"Dad, how did you pick up Walter?"

"He phoned Marian Garten. Before the connection was completed through the switchboard we knew where he was talking from. Forty-five seconds later the radio police in a car cruising along Amsterdam Avenue picked him up in the phone booth. What of it?"

"Oh," drawled Ellery, "I was just thinking that if Mr. Garten does repudiate the story—and I'll bet you a thousand to one he does, if you don't go easy on Walter—and if Walter sticks to his story, you've got a case that any good lawyer would shoot to little bits in twenty minutes. It's no good without a signed confession. If you'll parole Walter in my custody until—" he paused, smiled—"seven minutes after six tonight, I'll guarantee that the confession will be signed and that Walter will tell the whole truth."

CHAPTER XIII

ROUNDUP

AFTER SENDING Raymond Garten, in the custody of two detectives, back to the Tombs, Inspector Queen finally compromised with Ellery. He would take no chances with Walter Mathews. Whether or not Walter actually killed his uncle did not greatly matter. In law he was accessory after the fact, a principal in the murder. Knowing that a crime had been committed, he had aided and abetted the murderer with willful intent to defeat justice. The inspector would defer bringing charges against him until nine that night, if Ellery thought it would be helpful in getting Garten to sign a confession. Walter would remain under guard in his room.

To this Ellery promptly agreed.

"One more favor, Dad," he said. "Will you bring Mr. Garten back here at five-thirty?"

"Now, son, what are you up to?" The inspector looked sharply at him.

"I've a plan," Ellery murmured. "If you'll be here with Garten at that time I think I can promise you a signed confession. In the meantime I've a few details to attend to. Look here, Dad, I've something to show you." He took a notebook from his pocket, tore out a sheet. "Glance over that."

The inspector took the paper and began to read. In the left-hand margin were listed a sequence of hours and minutes beginning at three the afternoon before and ending at half past six. After each there was a brief statement of what had occurred at the time specified.

Thurs. P.M.
- 3:00 Rhodes arrives at Mathews house for signing of new will.
- 3:10 Rhodes leaves.
- 3:11 Rhodes readmitted by Carlotta E.
- 4:45 E.Q. leaves the Garten house with vanload of books.
- 5:04 Walter phones Marian from the Garten apt., asking her to come there.
- 5:05 E.Q. arrives at Garten apt.
- 5:10 Marian and Griswold leave the Garten house for the Garten apt.

158 THE PERFECT CRIME

5:15-25 Garten is at Mathews house.
5:20 Marian and Griswold arrive at Garten apt.
5:30 Griswold leaves the Garten apt. for Bloomingdale's.
5:35 Walter leaves the Garten apt. to see his uncle.
5:40 Mathews phones Rhodes to come.
5:43 Walter arrives at Mathews house.
5:50 Carlotta sees Garten in the Garten library.
5:58 Chauffeur and cook next door hear shot.
5:58-6:02 (?) Carlotta hears shot.
6:00 (?) Lee hears shot.
6:05 The Boston boat blows whistle.
6:06 Walter phones police headquarters.
6:07 He phones Marian.
6:10 Garten in cigar store near Madison and 57th St.
6:20 Garten picks up bags at his old house.
6:20 Griswold returns to Garten apartment.
6:30 Garten arrives at apt.

The times noted in some cases are approximate and, of course, I've had to put down what the various people reported. Still, I believe that the whole schedule is accurate to within a minute or two.

The inspector handed the paper back to Ellery.

"There's no news there for me, El," he said, unimpressed. "It's a good bookkeeping job and, as you say, accurate, as far as I can see. But what of it?"

"Just this, Dad. Taken in conjunction with the sketch

ROUNDUP

of this room—you know, the one I showed you yesterday—the schedule solves the entire mystery."

The inspector shook his head skeptically.

"It does, eh? And what has it got to do with my bringing Garten back here at five-thirty?"

"I'll explain then. I've never let you down, have I?"

Inspector Queen pursed his lips.

"All right. I'll have Garten here."

"Thanks, Dad," Ellery said, going to the kidney table to pick up the phone. He dialed a number.

"See you later." Briskly the inspector started off through the drawing room.

Ellery recognized the telephone operator's voice.

"Connect me with Mr. Garten's apartment, Caesar."

"Yas, suh. Just one minute, suh."

"Hello." Marian's voice.

"This is Ellery Queen."

"Mr. Queen! I'm almost frantic." Her voice was tense with distress. "They took Father away again. What does it mean? What are they doing to him?"

"Don't be upset," he said. "They'll just ask him a lot of questions, and he'll be back home presently."

"But are you sure that's all they want?"

"Yes."

"I'm so relieved! But—Walter called. I didn't have time to give him your message, though. He hung up in the middle of our conversation."

"What did he say before he hung up?"

"That I wasn't to think that he was guilty, but that he couldn't explain yet."

"Was that all?"

She hesitated.

"Well, he—said some personal things. Then suddenly he hung up."

"Probably disconnected," Ellery said cheerfully. "Don't worry about Walter, Marian. Is Griswold there?"

"Yes, do you want to speak to him?"

"Please."

"You'll call me later, won't you? I'm worried to death."

"I'll come up to see you at five. You'll be in?"

"Yes, of course. And thanks so very, very— Here's Mr. Griswold."

Griswold said, "Hello, Mr. Queen. What do the police want with Raymond Garten now? He told them everything he could yesterday, and Simpson, our lawyer, assured us Mr. Garten wouldn't be bothered again.

They were to communicate with him through Simpson."

"Is Marian close to the phone?" Ellery asked, lowering his voice.

"No, she's gone back to her room."

"Matters have taken a pretty serious turn, Mr. Griswold. I think it's best she shouldn't know until—well, until she has to be told."

"What's happened, Mr. Queen?" Griswold asked in a whisper.

"Raymond Garten has been charged with murder."

"That's absolutely preposterous!"

"Listen, Mr. Griswold. The story's bound to be in the afternoon papers. You mustn't let Marian see them. Be sure she doesn't go out. And tell the telephone operator that absolutely no calls are to be put through to your apartment after this one."

"Yes—yes, of course. You're quite right. I'll see to it," Griswold said, his voice shaking with agitation. "But the whole thing's nonsense, I tell you! I'll get Simpson on the job right away. I'll use an outside phone. I'll call from the drugstore at the corner."

"Just a minute, Mr. Griswold. Mr. Garten has made a complete confession. So I doubt very much if his lawyer will be allowed to see him before tomorrow."

There was a long silence. Then a scarcely audible whisper grated over the wire.

"*Confessed? Good God! What has he confessed?*"

"*To murdering John Mathews.*"

Griswold positively snorted.

"Do you know what it means, Mr. Queen? He's doing it to protect Walter Mathews—for Marian's sake!"

"Perhaps. I'll be up to see Marian about five. Will you be there?"

"Yes," said Griswold grimly. "What are you going to tell her? Confession! I'll swear they've all gone out of their minds!"

Ellery went up to Walter's room. Walter was sitting glumly beside the detective. When Ellery told him of Garten's confession, Walter was more apathetic than surprised, Ellery thought. For a moment or two Walter stared at his feet. Then he sighed, "The old idiot! This'll just about finish Marian. But he has guts—I'll say that for him."

"Walter, the best thing you can do for Marian is help me get you out of the mess you're in."

Walter seemed not to understand. He blinked at Ellery.

"I'm going to ask you a couple of questions," Ellery continued. "Whatever you say will be reported by Detective Flint and may be used against you. So use your head, and just answer yes or no, if you can. You can count on my knowing about everything that happened. There are only two facts I have to be sure of if you want me to help you—and Marian. You're in a tight spot, and don't forget it."

Flint shuffled his feet and looked disapproving. He'd got into enough trouble on this case already, and he didn't like all this talk.

"Look, Mr. Queen," he began, "I know you're the inspector's son, and—"

"Don't excite yourself, Flint," Ellery murmured. "I just told Mathews you'll report anything he says. Your hands are perfectly clean!" He turned back to Walter. "You threw something out the French window, didn't you, Walter—afterwards, I mean?"

Walter gaped. Then he nodded, looking completely mystified.

"Because of what you threw you had to wait for the

boat to pass before you telephoned the police—and me. Is that correct?"

Amazed, Walter stared at Ellery.

"Yes," he said, after a moment.

"I knew it," Ellery said calmly, "but I had to be sure. Now, did your uncle mention having phoned Rhodes a few minutes before you got here yesterday afternoon?"

Walter's whole expression revealed his incredulity.

"Yes. He told Rhodes that he'd call him back later and asked him to be sure to wait for the call. At least, that's what Uncle John told me he'd said."

Ellery sighed and put his hand lightly on Walter's shoulder.

"All right, Walter. It wouldn't be quite such a mess if you'd spilled even half the truth in the first place."

Leaving Walter, Ellery crossed the hall and knocked on Carlotta Emerson's door. After the click-clack-click of French heels, it opened, and she stood framed in the doorway, flaming red curls piled high on her head.

"May I come in a moment, Miss Emerson?" Ellery smiled. "I shan't trouble you for more than a minute."

"Eu, suahly, Mistah Queen. Come *right* in!" She smiled back at him as if he were Cary Grant.

Ellery sauntered over to the window opposite the door and looked out.

"Was it from here that you saw Mr. Garten in his library?"

"Eu, no, Mistah Queen. From *heah*," she said, going to the window to the left of the one where Ellery was standing.

He moved to her side. She used some kind of scent that was much too heavy.

"You're sure of the time? It was just ten minutes of six when you saw him?"

"That's right, Mistah Queen. Ah had just looked at mah watch and came to close the window."

"How was he dressed?"

"Dressed?" She fluttered a moment, as if it were too unladylike for her ever to notice what a male was wearing. Then she said carelessly, "Oh, he had on that maroon jacket he always wears in the house. Ah see him in the library often, you know."

"Did he have on his dark glasses?"

"Eu—why, yes, he did. He's been wearing them for a week or so now, constantly. He prob'ly strained his eyes. He's always readin'. That's all he evah does, as fah as Ah can make out."

"Where was Togo?" Ellery asked her abruptly.

She drew back from him. But her tone was as casual as ever.

"Togo?" she drawled. "Why, down in the garden or up on the roof, I suppose. He often goes up and down the pipe."

"But you say you closed the window. How could he get back into the house?"

"Oh, he'd come up the pipe and knock at the window. Or he'd come whenever I called him."

"I see. Thank you, Miss Emerson," smiled Ellery.

Arthur Rhodes's blonde receptionist stopped chewing her gum and took up the telephone receiver.

"Mr. Ellery Queen calling to see you," she said, stressing the "Ellery." She hung up and flashed her smile at him. "Go right in, Mr. Queen."

As Ellery went towards the door to Rhodes's private office, it opened.

"Come in, Queen!" Rhodes boomed. "What can we do for you today?" His overbearing manner had vanished, Ellery noticed, in a sort of nervous affability.

"When John Mathews telephoned you the last time, did he ask you to come and see him immediately or did he say he'd call you back later and that you were to wait here for the call?"

Before answering, Rhodes took a box of cigars from the desk drawer.

"Have one?" he asked cordially, holding the box towards Ellery.

Ellery shook his head.

"No, thanks."

"Well, as a matter of fact—" The lawyer stopped to light a cigar. "As a matter of fact, he did say something of the sort, but not quite that. You've got the emphasis wrong. He said he wanted to see me. I told him I was tied up for a while. Then he asked me to come over there later *unless* he called back. As I didn't hear from him, I went over."

"Is that what you told Inspector Queen?"

"Why, I don't know that I went into detail. As I recall it, I told your father that Mathews had sent for me and that I went to see him as soon as I could."

"Do you mind giving Inspector Queen the amended version of your telephone conversation?"

"Of course not," Rhodes said, but he frowned. "Why should I mind? I'll call him right now if you'd like." He reached for the phone on his desk.

"Not now, Mr. Rhodes. The inspector is not at his office. He told me to ask you to meet him at the Mathews house at five-thirty. The person who killed Mathews has been arrested."

The cigar almost fell.

"You don't say! Well, I'll be— Was it Walter, or aren't you at liberty to say?"

"Oh, there's nothing confidential about it. You'll see it in the papers in another hour or so. No, not Walter Mathews, but Raymond Garten."

"You don't say! Well, well! Of course, Garten had motive enough, I suppose."

"The inspector can count on your being there at five-thirty?"

"Absolutely. Absolutely. But I don't see that John's conversation with me has any bearing on the—"

"That's for Inspector Queen to judge, don't you think?" Ellery smiled as he rose to go.

"But, Ellery," Nikki asked as the cab drew up before the apartment house, "why are we going to the Gartens' if he's confessed? And why are you being so mysterious about everything?"

Consulting his watch, Ellery saw that it lacked one

minute of being five o'clock. So far everything had moved on schedule. The telephone at the Mathews house had been disconnected. It was impossible for Carlotta Emerson or Walter to get in touch with anyone outside, and Rhodes could not call Carlotta. Rhodes, moreover, was being watched, and if he did not start for the Mathews house by five-twenty he would be brought there. Then the detective the inspector had put at Ellery's disposal had rehearsed his part. All that remained now was to pick up Marian and Griswold.

"Are you in a trance, Ellery?" Nikki demanded. "Or is it lockjaw?"

"Wait here," he said, squeezing her hand as he opened the door of the cab. "I won't be more than a minute or two."

Caesar had announced Ellery, and Marian had the door of the apartment open before he was out of the elevator.

"Ellery," she asked anxiously, "have you any news? Have you seen Father?"

"I'll take you to see him now if you like," he said.

"If I like! Oh, Ellery—"

"The cab's waiting out in front."

"I'll be right back." She flew off.

In the sitting room, Ellery found Griswold massaging his foot and swearing in three ancient languages.

"Hurt yourself, Mr. Griswold?"

"No, no. It's nothing. My feet ache, that's all. I've been tramping the streets ever since you called. Did I hear you tell Marian that you're taking her to see Ray? I want to see him— The old fool! Confession!"

"Come along, by all means. You can bring Marian back home later, too."

"Good!" said Griswold, slipping his shoe on. "I'm anxious to see Ray. He won't lie to *me*! Besides his 'confession,' is there any evidence against him?"

"More than enough, I'm afraid—against him and against Walter."

"Well, it's all balderdash, Heaven knows," Griswold said irritably. "Raymond had told me where he went walking after he left Mr. Mathews. I've gone over the same route I don't know how many times this afternoon, showing his photograph to people! The men at the newsstands, storekeepers, and so forth. You'd think that surely someone would remember seeing him. The cigar-store man was the only—" Hearing Marian in the hall, he stopped abruptly and began to lace his shoe.

In the cab, after Ellery had introduced Nikki to Griswold and Marian, no one spoke until the car turned east on Fifty-seventh Street. Marian, between Nikki and Griswold in the rear seat, kept staring out the window, although she was unaware of anything on the street as the cab sped south. Her reddened eyelids suggested that she had been crying most of the afternoon. Griswold had shrunk back into the corner. He sat looking gloomily at his hands, which were folded on his lap. Nikki could not take her eyes off Ellery. What he had planned was a complete mystery to her. You never could tell about Ellery. At the moment, he was wholly absorbed in his thoughts, and from his brooding expression, she decided they were thoroughly unpleasant.

But when the cab turned east, Griswold asked in surprise, "Aren't we going to police headquarters, Mr. Queen?"

"No," Ellery said, "we're bound for the Mathews house. The crime was committed there, and it's there we must look for the solution."

"But, Ellery," Marian said, bewildered, "is Father there—at the Mathews house?"

"Yes." Ellery looked at her. "And Walter. I'm going

to ask you to trust me, Marian. What I've got to do won't be pleasant—for me or anyone else. I need your co-operation—your good sense."

The cab had stopped. Marian looked up at the Mathews house. The shades were drawn, and it had a deserted, forbidding look. Suddenly a tremor shook her body. Her hands trembled as Ellery helped her out of the cab.

CHAPTER XIV

THE MURDER AGAIN

"IT IS NOW exactly five-forty." Standing in the Mathews library with his back to the drawing-room doorway, Ellery Queen looked up from the watch on the palm of his hand.

Although the couch between the refectory table and the fireplace had been removed, and several small chairs, facing into the room, substituted for it, the other furnishings of the library were as they had been when Walter reported the death of John Mathews to the police.

Beside Ellery stood two detectives and Sergeant Velie. Inspector Queen was seated in one of the two upholstered chairs near the fireplace, and in the other, opposite him, Griswold.

The small straight chairs that took the place of the couch were arranged in two rows. In the back row was Marian, her father between her and Walter. Next to Walter at the end, near Ellery, sat Nikki. Only one of the seats in the front row was occupied. Arthur Rhodes sat on the last chair, as stiff as the ends of his handlebar moustache.

Everyone was tense, watching Ellery.

"You will remember," he said, turning towards Rhodes, "that at this time yesterday you were in your office, talking on the phone with Mr. Mathews."

Rhodes nodded.

"Twenty minutes before, about five-twenty, Miss Garten and Mr. Griswold arrived at the apartment uptown. After staying for ten minutes, Mr. Griswold left for Bloomingdale's. Walter, you left the apartment at five-thirty-five, to come here."

"I'll take your word for it," Walter said.

"You don't have to take my word for the time you got here," Ellery continued. "According to your own statement it was five-forty-three by the clock in the hall."

"That's right," he agreed.

"Now, Mr. Garten, I'm going to ask you to go with Sergeant Velie and do exactly what he tells you to.

The instructions he gives you may not entirely conform with your actions yesterday afternoon. However, please follow his instructions regardless of any minor discrepancies. To the best of my ability I am going to re-enact what happened yesterday between five-forty-three and seven minutes past six, when Walter telephoned to Miss Garten. All right, Mr. Garten, I'll ask you to go quickly."

Garten came forward. Velie took his arm and led him from the room. One of the detectives beside Ellery followed them. After a moment the others heard the front door close.

"Now, Walter, please do not make any suggestions or corrections while Hagstrom here," Ellery motioned towards the second detective, "plays the roll of John Mathews. He is going to enact my conception of what occurred in this room yesterday. I'm going to play your part. Please don't correct us if I'm wrong about your actions. You'll have the opportunity to do so later. I shall not try to repeat your conversation with your uncle. The performance is to be in pantomime, and occasionally I'll step out of your role to give directions and possibly ask some questions. No one will speak, please, unless he is spoken to."

The inspector's bright little eyes were watching Ellery. Rhodes sat up even more stiffly. Marian reached across the empty chair that her father had left between herself and Walter, to touch his arm. Without taking his eyes off Ellery, Walter moved over beside her as, with an expression of intense curiosity, Griswold moved forward to the edge of his chair.

"It is now exactly forty-three and a half minutes past five. You have already come through the drawing room, Walter, where you laid your hat on the settee. You have come in here." Ellery turned to the detective. "All right, Hagstrom."

The detective went quickly to the desk chair, beside which Mathews's body had lain, and sat down. Ellery crossed to the chair beside the kidney table.

"Dad," he said, looking at the inspector, "please, in your mind's eye, see Walter Mathews sitting here discussing certain matters with his uncle. Gradually, Walter becomes more angry. He is told that he has to break entirely with his fiancée or be disinherited. He finally threatens his uncle with exposure. Now, before proceeding, I'm afraid we'll have to wait for an absent witness."

"El," Inspector Queen demanded disapprovingly,

plucking at his straggly whiskers, "how long is this going to go on?"

"Until seven past six, Dad—or perhaps it won't be necessary to carry on that long." He looked down at his watch, which he still held in his hand. "It's nearly five-fifty now. The witness should be here presently. Please be patient—all of you."

In the tense silence that followed, only the slow ticking of the clock could be heard. To those waiting, the three minutes that passed before they heard footsteps in the hall seemed like twenty. Then came the clacking of heels on the parquet floor in the drawing room. A moment later Carlotta Emerson came through the doorway.

Nervous, she looked self-consciously about the room and then saw Ellery.

"Miss Emerson," he said, "will you please tell me exactly what you have been doing for the past ten minutes?"

"Mistah Queen, Ah've been doing just what you told me to."

"Which was?"

"Ah lay down on the bed and pretended Ah was taking a nap, the way Ah did yesterday."

"When did you get up?"

"At ten minutes to six, like you told me to. And Ah went and closed the window."

"What did you see?"

"Ah saw Mr. Garten back yonder in his lib'ary."

"What was he doing?"

"He was walkin' back and forth, that's all."

"Just as you saw him yesterday, at that time?"

"Just about, Ah guess, Mistah Queen."

"Thank you. Please take a seat with the others, Miss Emerson."

She crossed quickly and sat down beside Rhodes, without a glance towards those on the back row.

"It is now five-fifty-five," Ellery announced, as he got up from the chair by the kidney table and went back to stand in the doorway to the drawing room. He turned once more towards the inspector. "Dad, I'm assuming that the testimony of the cook and the chauffeur next door is correct. They said that they heard a shot at five-fifty-eight. That leaves me only two and a half minutes—so excuse me if I talk fast. Miss Emerson recalled hearing the shot at a little before or a little after six. Lee thought it was about six. Both had to approximate the time, judging it from the blowing of the whistle of the Boston boat, several minutes later. The exact time the pistol was fired is not of paramount importance. The approximate time is. And I'll ask you to remember that none of the four who heard the shot thought at the time they heard it that the sound came from this room. Lee thought he heard a car backfire on the Drive. Then Miss Emerson and the cook assumed that Mr. Garten was practicing in his basement. It was only after they were told that the pistol had been fired in this room that they concluded that it had been. As a matter of fact, it wasn't."

The inspector half rose from his chair.

"But that's impossible, Ellery. The only window through which Mathews could have been shot from outside was closed and locked. Besides, we know the bullet came from the opposite direction. And if he was shot from outside, we would have found either the bullet or the bullet hole if the bullet had been removed after passing through the neck."

Ellery held up his hand.

"Sorry, Dad. I can't stop to explain. I've only one minute left. . . . Walter has presumably gone upstairs.

He's taken his gloves and wrist watch from the bureau. He's coming into the drawing room now. Quick, Walter, come here. Quick."

White-faced, Walter hurried to Ellery. Ellery took him by the shoulders and turned him so that he faced the open French window.

"From here, Walter, you can see the last window at the east end of the Garten library, just as you can see it from the settee in the drawing room. Now, tell me what you see. Is the window open?"

"Yes," Walter mumbled.

"Do you see anyone in the library?"

"No! No! I won't! I won't!" Walter suddenly cried. "It's a lie. I didn't."

"Tell me what you see—now." Ellery dug his fingers into Walter's shoulders.

"I see Mr. Garten. But I didn't then." Walter's voice was subdued again.

"All right. What is he doing?"

"Looking down."

"At what?"

"A pistol." His shoulders began to shake violently.

"What's he doing to it?"

"Putting something on the barrel."

"Dad, remember, Hagstrom is John Mathews," Ellery snapped. "Ready, Hagstrom! Start. Move slowly."

The detective got up from Mathews's chair. He walked diagonally across the room and stopped before the refectory table to look down at the row of books at the back of it.

"What's Mr. Garten doing now, Walter? Speak, quick!"

Ellery felt Walter's body tremble.

"Aiming the pistol." The whisper was scarcely audible.

Hagstrom's arm reached out. He touched the book at the end of the row.

"Look out!" Walter shouted and flung himself to one side.

Simultaneously from the Garten library window came a flash and a loud report.

Hagstrom staggered backwards and fell at Ellery's feet. A red blotch on the rug under his neck began to spread out wider and wider.

Inspector Queen leaped to his feet. Marian Garten started screaming hysterically. Griswold, his mouth agape, stood up and stared down at Hagstrom. Carlotta frantically clutched Rhodes's arm. Rhodes, his stiffness gone, had slumped back on the chair, recoiling from the sight before him. Wide-eyed and pale, Nikki stared at Ellery.

Then Marian's screaming stopped as abruptly as it had started, for, not ten seconds after they had heard the pistol shot and seen Hagstrom fall, Raymond Garten, with Sergeant Velie holding his arm, came into the room. They all turned in bewilderment.

"But, but—" Walter stammered. "Why, but I saw you! Mr. Garten, weren't you—"

"No, Mr. Garten wasn't," Ellery said quietly. "And you didn't see him. That's just the point. And you didn't either, Miss Emerson," he murmured, "either yesterday or today. For the past fifteen minutes he's been with Sergeant Velie out in front on the sidewalk. Now, please be calm, everyone. Hagstrom's not hurt. That red stuff is ketchup, not blood. And a blank was fired in the Garten library. That's the main difference between yesterday's performance and today's." He turned to Velie. "You and Mr. Garten sit down with the others, please."

As Velie and Garten did so, Walter and Griswold resumed their seats. The inspector, however, remained standing. There was no mistaking his annoyance as he stood scowling at Ellery and blowing through his gray moustache.

"Ellery, the murderer was over by the table at the other end of the room. He's confessed, and all the details check with the material and circumstantial evidence—"

"Just a minute, Dad." Ellery spun on his heel. "Walter," he said sharply, "if you wish to keep Raymond Garten from going to the electric chair, you'll tell the truth now! Was your uncle's body when you found it in about the position that Detective Hagstrom is in now?"

Walter glanced down at the detective, who had not moved after falling to the floor.

"As nearly as I can remember," he said.

"Mr. Garten, did you shoot John Mathews from the window of your library?"

"Of course not. I—"

"That's enough, thank you." Ellery turned back to Walter. "Did you see someone in the Garten library fire the shot that killed your uncle?"

To the inspector's astonishment Walter nodded.

He swallowed hard and said, "Yes. Yes, I did."

"Very well. Now I'm going to show you what you

did after you saw the murder. You believed that Mr. Garten had done it. You loathed your uncle and thought he deserved what he got. You certainly weren't going to let the father of the girl you loved go to the electric chair for an act that you considered a blessing to mankind." Ellery reached into his pocket and took out a pair of suède gloves. "These are yours, Walter. You put them on to avoid leaving fingerprints. You planned to move Mathews's body to a place in which he could not have been shot from outside, but only by someone in the room. The someone was to be Mathews himself. It was to look like suicide. But then you saw that you couldn't move the body without revealing that you had done so, because the rug was stained at this end. It would have been impossible to wash out the stain, even if you'd had all the time you wanted. Then you got an idea. You probably turned up the edge of the rug and saw that the blood hadn't soaked through to the floor yet." Ellery went to the other end of the room and moved the chair beside which the body had been lying when he first saw it.

"Now, this is what you did next."

He grasped the rug at the corner before the French window and, pulling it so that Hagstrom was dragged with it, reversed its position. He then moved the chair back to its customary place and, going to the table by the window, took a pistol from the drawer. "This is not the same pistol, but it will do. Incidentally, there's only one cartridge in it, and it's a blank. Naturally, you wouldn't present a very convincing picture of suicide if you placed a fully-loaded pistol that had never been fired beside the hand of the dead man. But if you fired it to complete the suicide picture, the shot would be heard by Miss Emerson upstairs, possibly by Lee, and undoubtedly by the two servants in the kitchen downstairs, and someone would be bound to come rushing in. That wouldn't do at all. You wanted to be out of here before the body was discovered, and you couldn't take the chance of being seen running away immediately after the pistol was fired. Then you got another idea that solved that problem. But you missed two vital points. The first was that the leg of the chair beside which your uncle was then lying had made a deep impression in the chenille of the rug. After you turned the rug around, the impression was of course at the corner diagonally opposite the chair. You'll notice now that the leg of the chair is once more in the impression that it made.

"Since the rug had been turned round the reason for its reversal was obvious to me. Mathews was standing somewhere near the diagonally opposite corner from the desk. The book, *Wills and Testaments,* sticking out several inches beyond the others, suggested that he was in the act of taking it when he was killed. He had wills and testaments very much on his mind yesterday. Moreover, the book would be within his reach if he'd been standing where he fell, as shown by the stain on the rug. In other words, the body's position with respect to the rug had not been changed. When you've reasoned so far, it immediately becomes obvious that the bullet came from the direction of the French window, as it passed from left to right through the neck. But where did the bullet go? Fortunately, from your point of view, Walter, it struck the safe by the door. In my diagram, Dad," Ellery glanced towards his father, "I marked the spot where the paint is chipped off the safe. Walter, you picked up the flattened bullet and threw it across the fence, against the wall of the Garten house. You reasoned that if it was found the police would surmise that the bullet had gone out the window. However, as we see now, a straight line from the east window of the Garten library to the mark on the safe passes about five feet above the floor where Mathews was standing.

"The other thing you overlooked, Walter, was the powder burns. Had you thought of them and fired the pistol—when you finally got around to doing so—so that powder marks would have been left on Mathews's neck, his death would probably have been accepted as suicide. Too bad you didn't think of that. It couldn't have taken more than two or three minutes at most to set the suicide stage. And it wasn't until six-five that you fired the pistol."

Ellery again looked at his watch. It was four and a half minutes after six.

"Why, El, did he wait before firing the pistol?" The inspector seemed finally convinced by Ellery's demonstration and logic. "I don't see what he gained by waiting."

"Because he wanted to minimize the chances of the shot's being heard. After he fired, he ran to the front door and saw the butler outside. He knew that Lee would be coming downstairs in another minute. He was trapped and did the only thing he could in the circumstances. Pretended that he'd found the body—"

"That's what I've said right along. But why did he have to wait?" Inspector Queen interrupted.

Ellery Queen turned to face the French window and pointed the pistol towards the Garten house.

"You'll have the answer to that in ten seconds, Dad." Ellery paused and then said, "In four seconds it'll be five after."

They listened to the tick of the clock on the mantel.

Then came the loud blast of the Boston boat's whistle.

Ellery pressed the trigger. A streak of flame shot from the pistol.

"Wait quietly, please," he said, turning towards the doorway to the drawing room.

The others turned, their gaze following his, their curiosity becoming more intense with each dragging second. After a few minutes someone could be heard shuffling across the hall, across the drawing room.

Then Lee appeared in the doorway. He stopped short and looked first at Ellery and then at Walter.

"No," he said after a moment, "he not theah. He at telephone, asking 'Hully, please.'"

"Never mind, Lee," Ellery said. "Did you hear a pistol shot?"

The Chinese nodded.

"At what time?"

"Two minute before six o'clock."

"Did you hear a second shot?"

"No. One shot. Then I wait; steamboat blow whistle. Then I come down."

"Say, Mr. Queen," Sergeant Velie interposed, "our yellow friend could have got himself up to look like Mr. Garten. Don't forget that Mathews swindled him, too. Why did he stick around after the other servants left? He'd have had plenty of time to get back to the room."

Ellery shook his head.

"Obviously someone put on Mr. Garten's maroon coat and a pair of dark glasses—the disguise would be convincing enough in the twilight, as we've seen; if 'Mr. Garten' were seen, what harm? It was his house! The detective who wore the maroon coat and sun glasses this afternoon convinced both Miss Emerson and Walter that he was Mr. Garten. But the murderer wasn't Lee, and if Walter hadn't messed things up for him, he might have got away with it. Before I name the murderer, though, there's something I'd like Miss Emerson to know." He stepped towards her and Rhodes. "Rhodes, you have Mr. Mathews's last will in your safe, have you not?"

Rhodes licked his lips.

"Yes."

"It leaves everything to Miss Emerson."

"Yes."

"She will then receive the entire estate regardless of whether she marries you or not?"

"Naturally," he said, turning red and pulling himself up haughtily. "What business of yours is that?"

"None," Ellery admitted blandly, "though perhaps it's news to Miss Emerson. Now, please have the grace to tell the truth about Mr. Mathews's last phone call. Didn't he say that Walter had just phoned him and that there was a possibility of a reconciliation between them, and that if he could bring Walter round to his way of thinking, he would reinstate the old will?"

Suddenly Carlotta recoiled from Rhodes in horror.

"You—you *liar*!" she shrieked. "You—it was *you*—"

"Wait a minute," Inspector Queen interrupted, coming forward. "El, are you accusing Rhodes of the murder?"

"No, Dad. I'm not."

"Then who in blazes did do it?"

"The murderer of John Mathews," Ellery said slowly, "is dead—I hope. I suspect that he has taken the easier way out. A few minutes ago he slipped something into his mouth. He knew his number was up. Look, Dad, behind you."

Inspector Queen spun around.

Eyes closed, face a gray white, yet with an expression of peace, hands limply lying on an envelope in his lap, his head resting against the back of the chair, Henry Griswold sat as though he had dozed off quietly.

Ellery crossed to the chair by the fireplace and picked up the envelope. It was addressed: "To Ellery Queen." He opened the envelope and took out a sheet of paper covered with neat handwriting. After a moment he handed it to the inspector.

"His confession. When I phoned just after Mr. Garten told you that he was guilty of the murder, Griswold suspected I might be giving him his chance. He took it."

CHAPTER XV

DICTATION

IN ELLERY QUEEN's private office the following morning, Nikki Porter sat beside his desk, her stenographic book in her lap.

"But why this sudden rush to dictate?" she demanded, inspecting the sharp point of her pencil.

"We've got to make up for lost time. Wait a minute." He picked up the sheets of paper in the OUT basket and glanced through them. "I'm in the middle of Chapter Eight. Ready, Nikki?"

Nikki's forehead wrinkled.

"No," she said, and put down her pencil. "This is a strike."

"A strike?"

"Yes. I'm not going to do a lick of work until you tell me the rest of the Griswold story!"

Ellery leaned back in his chair, looking murderous. Then he sighed. She wouldn't concentrate on what he dictated and would get it all balled up. He might as well tell her and be done with it.

"All right, Nikki," he said impatiently. "Then full steam ahead. Agreed?"

She nodded eagerly.

"When Marian and Griswold arrived at the Garten apartment—after I'd delivered the books in the van, that is—there was an envelope addressed to Ray Garten on the table. As I told you, Marian told Griswold to open it, and he did. I noticed at the time that it contained a note and what looked like a deposit slip. Later I found out that it was a deposit slip. Remember my telling you about Garten's interview with Mathews? Mathews had deposited $200,000 to Garten's credit at the bank so that it would look as if Garten had been in on the swindle from the start. Garten told me about it in Griswold's presence after the murder. Up to then Griswold thought—just as Mathews intended everyone should think, if Garten sicked the D.A. onto him—that he, Garten, was in league with Mathews to fleece the stockholders. Among the stockholders, with his life savings invested, was Griswold. When he saw the deposit slip he was convinced that he'd been betrayed in the nastiest sort of way by his old friend Garten. Garten, with the show he'd been putting on about losing everything, was a worse villain than Mathews in Griswold's mind. Probably at the time he imagined that John Mathews, Walter, and Garten were all in on the swindle together. There was not only the $200,000 deposit, but the check I'd given Garten on Walter's behalf. Moreover, Garten still had his library. The whole transaction, as Griswold must have seen it, was a blind to cover Garten's role in the swindle."

Ellery swung his chair round so that he could look out the window.

"Oh, of course," Nikki exclaimed. "So Griswold pretended he was going to get that stuff at Bloomingdale's and—"

"He stopped off there and bought the saddle soap," Ellery interrupted. "Naturally he would, in order to have an alibi of sorts. But he left the apartment at five-thirty and didn't get back until six-twenty, so it wasn't much of one, at that. He wanted to kill two birds with one stone—Garten and Mathews. He paced up and down with Garten's maroon coat and some dark glasses on until Carlotta Emerson saw him. If Walter hadn't changed everything around, the police would have known at once where the murderer shot from. He knew they'd find the bullet and the ballistics experts would prove that it had been fired from Garten's gun. So after killing Mathews, Griswold put the pistol in Garten's bag and replaced the maroon coat. It was a bad break for him that the bullet hit the safe and was mutilated, but to make things worse, Walter heaved it over the fence. Anyhow, on the way home Griswold phoned the police to search Garten's apartment so they'd find the pistol; and to pile up more evidence against Garten, he conspicuously hid Garten's telescopic sight in the coal bin."

"You mean it was Griswold who climbed up on the coal in the night while you were in the Garten house?"

"It was Griswold, all right. But he wasn't putting it there then. He was trying to get it back when the coal shifted under him and he heard me coming to the basement."

"But what did he want it back for?" Nikki demanded.

It was a moment or two before Ellery answered. He sat gazing out the window, lost in thought.

"Don't you see, Nikki," he said at last, "in the meantime he'd found out what a ghastly mistake he'd made. He'd learned the truth about the $200,000 deposit and about Mr. Garten! He must have been pretty bewildered at first by the proceedings, because the chances are that he beat it the moment he fired and so would not have seen Walter changing things around. But later he must have realized that Walter had seen him and mistaken him for Garten! I think he would have confessed rather than let either of them pay for his crime—once he knew that Garten and Walter were not confederates of Mathews in the Chickawassi swindle."

"So you phoned him to tip him off?"

"I thought it was the best way out of the mess for everyone."

"And what about Walter? Will he be prosecuted?"

"No. Dad says the whole story—as far as Walter's concerned—will be buried in the public archives."

"Is he going to marry Marian soon?" Nikki asked, brightening.

"Yes, next month."

"And is Carlotta going to marry the man with the moustache—what's his name—Rhodes?"

Ellery's thoughts again seemed to be drifting out the window.

"Well?" Nikki demanded.

"She gave Rhodes the air—and half the Mathews estate to Walter. All right?"

"Oh, I think that's fine!"

"All right, then?"

"What do you keep saying 'all right' for? Of course it's all right."

Apparently Ellery did not hear. Several moments passed before he spoke again.

"Darling—"

"Yes, Ellery."

"Darling, there's something I've wanted to tell you for a long time now." He paused. "But crime—how fate seems eternally to interpose crime between us! . . . But now—now at last, my darling—" Again he paused.

Nikki's eyes had become as round and as bright as new silver quarters. She leaned forward and smiled mistily, happily, at Ellery's broad back.

"How about it, Nikki?"

"Yes, Ellery. Oh, yes!" She was ready to fall into his arms. *Dear* Ellery! How he'd concealed his feelings towards her. . . .

"Then for the love of Sherlock Holmes," roared Ellery, turning around, "forget the Mathews case and let's get back to work!"